'Anyone wou [*want me to* **?**] ***yineka mou,*** **Angelos drawled.**

Anyone would be right. Her body grew rigid as the full import of his comment penetrated. 'Move in?' Georgette echoed sharply.

'I think we should start as we mean to go on. We did agree that this is to be a marriage in every sense of the word.'

'That would be sensible...the starting as you mean to go on bit, I mean,' she agreed cautiously. 'But unfortunately my flat is tiny—one bedroom.'

'Cosy,' he replied. 'I'll see you in the bedroom...'

Kim Lawrence lives on a farm in rural Anglesey. She runs two miles daily and finds this an excellent opportunity to unwind and seek inspiration for her writing! It also helps her keep up with her husband, two active sons, and the various stray animals which have adopted them. Always a fanatical consumer of fiction, she is now equally enthusiastic about writing. She loves a happy ending!

PREGNANT BY THE GREEK TYCOON

BY
KIM LAWRENCE

MILLS & BOON®

*First published in Great Britain 2005
Harlequin Mills & Boon Limited,
Eton House, 18-24 Paradise Road, Richmond, Surrey TW9 1SR*

© Kim Lawrence 2005

ISBN 0 263 84150 2

*Set in Times Roman 10¼ on 11½ pt.
01-0505-50419*

*Printed and bound in Spain
by Litografia Rosés, S.A., Barcelona*

CHAPTER ONE

'OF COURSE I knew it would never last.'

The words brought Georgie to an abrupt halt as she was dragged back four years in time without warning.

For most people it had been the summer of the heatwave, when cold, damp Britain had basked in tropical temperatures. For Georgie it had been the summer her life had changed.

She had been just twenty-one then, a fairly typical student enjoying the summer break before returning to college for her final year. Her only plans had revolved around the teaching career she'd wanted and the car she'd been saving up to buy.

The previous term she had been stopped in the street by a clipboard-wielding woman doing a survey for a television programme.

'Do you believe in marriage?'

'I don't *disbelieve* in it.'

'So you would get married?' the interviewer pressed.

'Me...? Oh, I'm far too young to be even thinking about it.' Georgie laughed. 'I want to have some fun before I settle down.'

Barely three months later she had been exchanging vows with a man she had known less than a month.

And yes, her grandmother *had* told her it would never last, but this had hardly put her in an exclusive category! It would have been hard to find someone who *had* thought the marriage was a good idea!

Georgie, floating several feet off the ground, had smiled serenely through the lectures and totally ignored the predictions of disaster. If anything the opposition had stiffened her resolve, made it seem somehow more romantic to her.

Her lips twisted in a self-derisive grimace as she recalled the idyllic future she had seen stretching ahead of her.

'Mummy…!'

Georgie pushed aside the memories crowding in on her and turned to the little boy who was holding up some treasure in his chubby hand for her to admire. Long, curling lashes as black as the glossy curls that covered his head lifted from his rosy cheeks as he raised his cherubic, smiling face to hers.

Not everything that had come from her ill-judged marriage had been negative. She had Nicky; she had her baby. Not that he was such a baby any longer, she thought ruefully as she made the appropriate admiring noises.

As Nicky went back to his game—he really was an extraordinarily contented, sunny child—Georgie banged the sandals she was carrying loudly against the wrought-iron table set on the patio.

It didn't have the desired effect. Too engrossed in their conversation, the women inside remained oblivious to her presence.

This is just what I need! A front-row seat to the dissection of the marriage from hell. Georgie could have saved them the bother; *bad idea* about summed it up.

'Were they together long?' Georgie recognised the distinctive Yorkshire accent of Ruth Simmons, a retired headmistress and keen bird-watcher who had rented the cottage next door to theirs for the summer.

'Six months.'

The way her grandmother said it made it sound like a jail sentence.

'Do you think there's any possibility of reconciliation?' the other woman probed. 'Perhaps if they had given it more time…tried a little harder…?'

'Tried harder…what would be the point?'

Georgie leaned her forehead against the frame of the door and absently rubbed a flake of peeling paint with her thumb.

She was rarely in tune with her grandmother, but on this occasion she agreed totally with the older woman's reading of the situation. She could have spent half her life trying to be what Angolos wanted and she wouldn't have succeeded.

In the end, however, the choice to call it quits had not been hers.

Angolos had ended it. He had done so with brutal efficiency, but then, she reflected, Angolos didn't like to leave loose ends, and he was not sentimental.

'They could,' she heard her grandmother, Ann, reveal authoritatively, 'have tried until doomsday and the result would have been the same.'

'But *six months*…poor Georgie…'

The genuine sadness in the other woman's voice brought a lump of emotion to Georgie's throat. There hadn't been much sympathy going begging when she had swallowed her pride and turned up on her dad's doorstep. Plenty of, 'I told you so,' and a truck-load of, 'You've made your own bed,' but sympathy had been thin on the ground.

'With those two, it was never a matter of *if*, just *when* they would split up. *When* he got bored or *when* she woke up to the fact they came from different worlds. Far better that they cut their losses. He was only ever playing.'

It had felt pretty real to her at the time, but maybe Gran was right. *Were you playing, Angolos?* Sometimes she just wished she could have him in the same room for five minutes so that she could make him tell her *why*. Why had he done what he did?

'By all accounts his first wife led him quite a dance… beautiful, spirited, fiery…*apparently* she could have had a successful career as a concert pianist if she had dedicated as much energy to that as she did partying.

'In *my* opinion after the divorce he was looking for a new wife who could give him a quiet life…unfortunately he picked

Georgie. Inevitably the novelty wore off when he got bored with quiet and biddable.'

It was not an ego-enhancing experience to hear yourself described as what was basically a doormat. Sadly Georgie couldn't dispute the analysis. She had been pathetically eager to please, and it was awfully hard to relax and be yourself around someone you worshipped, and she had worshipped Angolos.

'I think you're doing Georgie an injustice,' Ruth protested. 'She's a bright, intelligent girl.'

Georgie leaned her shoulders against the wall, smiling to herself. Thank you, Ruth.

'Of course she is, but…look, let me show you this.'

Georgie could hear the sound of rustling and knew immediately what her grandmother was doing.

'This was in last week's Sunday supplement. *That* is Angolos Constantine.'

Georgie knew what the other woman was being shown; she had seen the magazine before her grandmother had hidden it under the cushions on the sofa. A double-page glossy picture showing Angolos stepping out of a chauffeur-driven car onto the red carpet of a film première. At his side was Sonia, his glamorous ex-wife. Were they back together…? Good luck to them, Georgie thought viciously. They deserved one another.

'Oh, my…!' she heard the older woman gasp. 'He really is quite…yes, *very*…! They do say opposites attract…' she tacked on weakly.

Nice try, Ruth, thought Georgie.

'There are opposites, and then there is Angolos Constantine and my granddaughter.'

Georgie's lips curved in a wry smile. You could always rely on her grandmother to introduce a touch of realism.

'It was always an absurd idea. She was never going to fit into his world, and they had nothing in common whatsoever except possibly…' Ann Kemp lowered her voice to a confidential whisper. It had a carrying quality that only someone who was a leading light of amateur dramatics could achieve.

'*Sex!* Or *love*, as my granddaughter preferred to call it. Personally I blame it all on those romances she read in her teens,' she confided.

'I'm partial to a good romance myself,' the other woman inserted mildly.

'Yes, but you're not a foolish, impressionable young girl who expects a knight in shining armour to come riding to the rescue.'

'Young, no, but I haven't totally given up hope.'

Georgie missed the dry retort.

A distracted expression stole over her soft features as she rubbed her bare upper arms, which, despite the heat, had broken out in a rash of goose bumps. Low in her pelvis the muscles tightened. She blinked hard to banish the image that had flashed into her head, but like the man it involved it didn't respond to her wishes, or even, she thought, her soft mouth hardening, her entreaties.

In the end, bewildered and scared, she had lost all dignity and begged him to reconsider. He *couldn't* want her to go away. They were happy; they were going to have a baby. 'Tell me what's wrong,' she had pleaded.

Angolos had not said anything, he'd just looked down at her, his midnight eyes as hard as diamonds.

Strange how one decision could alter the course of your life.

In her case, if she hadn't caved in to her stepbrother's nagging and taken him down to the beach, when she had actually planned to curl up in an armchair and finish the last chapter in her book, she would never have met Angolos. Not that there was any point speculating about what might have been.

You just had to live with what was, and Georgie thought in all modesty that she wasn't making such a bad job of it. She had good career, rented her own flat, a gorgeous son. A single friend had remarked recently that she didn't know how Georgie managed to cope being a single parent with a young child and a full-time, demanding job.

'I couldn't imagine my life without Nicky; he's the reason I do cope,' Georgie explained. It was true—not that her friend had believed a word of it.

The fact there was no man in her life was a matter of choice. Not that she had ruled out the possibility of meeting someone; she just couldn't imagine it.

Sometimes she tried to. She tried to imagine another man touching her the way Angolos had. She did now, and it was a mistake. Her nerve endings started to ache as she thought of his long, cool fingers on her skin.

Angolos had made her ache a lot.

When she wasn't thinking about Angolos's ability to make her ache, she occasionally wondered what sort of person she might have been if she had never met him. Would she still be as naïve and trusting as she had been that summer?

Such speculation was pointless, because she *had* met him, and every detail of that fateful occasion, the moment she had laid eyes on Angolos Constantine, the moment her life had changed for ever, was burnt into her brain.

She had been sitting on a blanket, one eye on the paperback she had been trying to finish and the other on her stepbrother, who had been playing with a group of boys farther down the beach. His shoes had been the first thing she had seen, shiny, hand-tooled leather, and then the exquisitely tailored legs of his dark trousers, expensive, tasteful, and *wildly* inappropriate for a beach.

She'd just had to see who would be stupid enough to venture onto the beach in a get-up like that! Georgie had lifted a hand to shade her eyes, squinting against the sun as her glance had travelled upwards.

Oh, my goodness…!

The owner of the shoes had had long legs, very long legs;

the rest of him had been a lot better than OK too. In fact, if you went for lean and hard—and what woman wouldn't, given half the chance?—he was as close to perfect as damn it.

By the time she had reached his face the last shreds of amused mockery had vanished from her amber eyes—*the eyes he had professed to love*—and she had been smitten and had stayed that way until the day he had told her he wanted her to go away.

'Go away…?' Uneasy, but sure this was all a silly mistake, she had asked, 'How long for?'

'For ever,' he had replied and walked away.

But on that first summer's afternoon there had been no hint of the casual cruelty he was capable of. She had been totally overwhelmed and too inexperienced to hide it as she'd stared back into those dark eyes shaded by preposterously long lashes that had thrown a shadow across the prominent angle of his chiselled cheekbones.

Those seductive, velvety depths had held a cynical world-weariness that her impressionable self had found fascinating, but then she'd found everything about him fascinating, she reflected grimly, from his sable-smooth hair to the mobile curve of his sensual lips.

Tall and lean, darkly arresting, his olive-skinned face an arrangement of strong angles and fascinating bone structure, he was the essence of male beauty.

'Hello,' he said, flashing her a seriously gorgeous smile. Like his appearance his voice with its faint accent marked this most rampantly *male* of males out as fascinatingly different.

She was hot, her face was sticky, her skin was glossed with a film of sweat and the salty dampness had gathered in the valley between her breasts. The jacket casually slung over one shoulder was the only concession this stranger made to the heat, which appeared not to affect him.

She lifted a self-conscious hand to her hair and discovered

it was full of salt from an earlier dip in the sea. She wanted desperately to be cool and say something intelligent but all she could manage was a breathless, 'Hello.' Her heart was beating so fast she could barely hear her own voice.

She knew she was staring, but she couldn't help it. She simply couldn't tear her eyes off this incredible man. Men like this did not walk down the beach of an old-fashioned family resort… She hadn't actually believed they existed outside the pages of popular fiction!

Did wondering what a total stranger looked like naked make her depraved? This had never happened to her before; maybe it was the weather? Hadn't she read somewhere that heat had an effect on the libido? But her libido had never given her any problems; in fact she had occasionally wondered if it wasn't a little underdeveloped.

'I'm not familiar with the area.'

'I know…'

One darkly defined brow lifted and she rushed on in hot-faced explanation.

'This is a small place and strangers…well, they stand out.' In the most fashionable and glamorous watering holes on the planet he would have stood out! She couldn't imagine what it would feel like to walk into a room and have heads turn and conversations stop. *What would he feel like?*

She lowered her gaze. Stop this, Georgie!

'Then you live here?'

He's talking to me. This incredible man is actually talking *to me*. What did he say…?

'Sorry?'

'Do you live locally?'

'Yes…no.'

The creases around his stupendous eyes deepened. 'Which?'

Oh, no, he was going to go back to whatever planet he came from—clearly he was too gorgeous to be earthbound—

and laugh about the mentally challenged locals. She made a supreme effort to act as though her IQ reached double figures.

'We spend the summer holidays here. My…' Her eyelashes lowered, as she repressed the embarrassing impulse to give him her life story. Even if that life could be summed up in a paragraph, his stupendous eyes would have glazed over with boredom before she got to the end.

One noteworthy thing had happened in her life and she didn't even remember it! She had been a baby when her mother had run away with a Greek waiter. Since then her deserted father had refused to travel abroad, hence the house here where she had spent every summer she could remember, firstly with just her father and grandmother, latterly with her stepmother and stepbrother.

'But you know the area well? You know all the places to go?'

'Places to go…?' Her puzzled expression cleared. 'I suppose I do.' She was delighted to be able to be of use to this most amazing man. 'Well, actually, it depends,' she told him seriously.

'On what?'

'If you have a head for heights.'

'I do.'

'Not me,' she admitted regretfully. 'The headland walk along the nature reserve is apparently marvellous, but if you prefer something a little gentler the trail across the marsh is very well marked and there are hides where you can… Are you interested in birds?' The area drew a lot of people who were; they arrived with their binoculars in their droves. 'It's not the breeding season, but there are still some—'

'I am not a bird-watcher; I prefer more…active pursuits.'

Now that he said it she had no problem seeing him fitting into the mould of those tough, reckless individuals who indulged in extreme sports… Extreme as in those *extremely* likely to result in injury or worse!

The thought of him breaking his beautiful neck made her unthinkingly blurt out, 'You should be careful.'

'At the moment I'm under strict instructions to relax.' A slow smile that made her tummy flip spread across his lean features. 'And suddenly,' he confided in a husky drawl that made Georgie's skin prickle, 'that doesn't seem such a bad idea.'

Was he flirting with her…? Georgie dismissed the thought even before it was fully formed.

'I was actually wondering about the night-life…?' he went on.

'Night-life?' she parroted. The distracting shadow of dark body hair visible through the fine fabric of his shirt was making it hard for her to concentrate on what he was saying.

'As in nightclubs.'

'*Nightclubs?*' she echoed as though he were talking a foreign language. 'Here?'

His beautifully moulded lips quirked. 'No nightclubs.' She shook her head. 'Restaurants…?'

Georgie's eyes had got even wider. 'I think you might have got the wrong place. There's the teashop next to the post office—they do a great cream tea—and the fish and chip shop, but… Are you laughing at me?'

'You're delightful.'

Even though she realised he probably meant delightful in a cutesie, cuddly, clumsy puppy sort of way, she couldn't stop smiling.

'And this feels like the first time I've laughed in a very long time.'

Georgie was pondering this enigmatic statement when a football landed in her lap, spraying sand all over her. There was the sound of laughter as she sprawled inelegantly backwards onto the sand.

'Jack Kemp!' she yelled, spitting out a mouthful of sand

as her stepbrother approached. She struggled into an upright position and glared at the guilty figure.

'What's got into you?' asked the freckle-faced twelve-year-old. 'It wasn't hard,' he added scornfully.

Clicking her tongue, she threw the ball back, with an admonition to be careful. 'And five minutes only,' she cautioned, glancing at her watch. 'I promised I'd get dinner tonight,' she reminded him.

'Sure…sure, Georgie,' Jack called back before loping off down the sand.

'Georgie…?'

'Georgette,' she said with a grimace. 'My family call me Georgie. That's my stepbrother,' she explained, nodding to the skinny running figure.

She turned as she spoke and found he wasn't looking at the distant figure of the fair-headed boy, but at her. There was a sensual quality in his dark-eyed scrutiny that sent a secret shiver through her body; the condition of her nipples was less a secret as they pressed against the stretchy fabric of her bikini top.

She looked around red-cheeked and mortified for the shirt she had discarded. She found it in a crumpled heap under the sun cream; hastily she fought her way into it.

'I will call you Georgette,' he pronounced.

She was never going to see him again, but as far as Georgie was concerned this man could call her anything.

CHAPTER TWO

'How old are you, Georgette?'

Georgie flirted briefly with the notion of coming back with a cool, *Old enough,* but she knew she'd never carry it off. Besides, how mortifying would it be if he laughed?

'Twenty-one,' she responded more conventionally.

'Will you come to dinner with me?' he asked without skipping a beat.

Her eyes, round with astonishment, flew to his. *'Me... you...?'*

'That was the general idea.'

Georgie swallowed before running her tongue over her dry lips—they tasted salty—and she looked at him suspiciously. 'You're not serious.' She tried to laugh but her vocal muscles didn't co-operate.

'Why would I not be?' She shook her head, flushing as his gaze became ironic. 'You are the most attractive woman on the beach.'

'I'm the only one under sixty without a husband and children,' she rebutted huskily, 'so I'll try not to get carried away with the compliment.'

Who was she kidding? Her entire life she had thought of herself as an average sort of girl—hidden depths, sure, but was anybody ever going to bother looking? Now totally out of left field there came this incredible man who was looking at her as though she were a desirable woman.

Carried away...? She was quite frankly blown away!

She tried to adopt an amused expression and failed miserably as the screen of ebony lashes swept up from his cheekbones. *Combustible* best described his smoky-eyed stare.

'I don't even know your name,' she protested weakly.

His smile had been confident, tinged with the arrogance that came naturally to someone like him. And why shouldn't it be? she mused, four years down the line. Angolos Constantine was used to getting what he wanted; a little bit of complacence was understandable when women had been falling at his feet since the day he'd hit puberty!

'Not an insuperable barrier and I already know yours, *Georgette.*' The way he said her name had a tactile quality. It made the hairs on her nape stand on end and intensified the unspecified ache low in her belly.

She stared back at him dreamily.

It was just dinner.

'It's just dinner,' he said as if he could read her thoughts.

What was she doing, hesitating? All the girls she knew wouldn't have needed coaxing. They saw what they wanted and went for it. Georgie applauded them, but privately wondered if in secret they weren't just as insecure as she was.

When she opened her mouth she intended to say yes, but her dad hadn't raised a reckless child. Caution had been drilled into her from her infancy, and at the last second her conditioning kicked in.

'Thank you, but I couldn't.' He was a total, a *total* stranger who could, for all she knew, be a psycho or even a *married* psycho. She shook her head; she was out of her depth and she knew it. 'Thank you, but I'm afraid I can't. My boyfriend wouldn't like it.'

Under other circumstances the look of baffled frustration on his lean face would have been laughable.

Georgie didn't feel like laughing; she didn't even feel like smiling. She was actually pretty ambivalent about the entire 'done the right thing' situation.

His dark brows lifted. 'Are you saying no?'

She could hear the astonishment in his voice and she realised that being knocked back had never crossed his mind. *No* was obviously not a word this man was used to hearing.

She nodded.

This time there was a hint of annoyance in his appraisal. 'As you wish.'

His irritation made her feel slightly better. Her normal nature, the one she had when she wasn't turned into a brainless bimbo by the sexual aura this man radiated, briefly reasserted itself. Why should he assume she was a sure thing? She might have been a bit *obvious*, but a girl could look without necessarily wanting to touch…

She flashed a quick semi-apologetic smile in his general direction. She wasn't trying to strike a blow for female equality here—better and braver women had already done that— she just wanted to get the hell out of there without making herself look any more a fool than she already had!

Aware that his disturbing eyes were following her actions as she crammed her possessions in her canvas bag made her clumsy.

'Jack!' she bellowed, zipping up the bag with a sigh of relief.

'You forgot this.'

She half turned and saw he was holding out a tube of sunblock.

She extended her hand. 'Thank you.' The fingertip contact lasted barely a heartbeat but it was enough to send an electrical tingle through her body. Her wide, startled eyes lifted momentarily to his and she knew without him saying a word that he knew exactly what she was feeling.

Well, at least someone did!

Without waiting to see if her aggravating stepbrother was following her, Georgie stumbled and ran across the sand to the pebbly foreshore, all the time fighting an insane impulse to turn back.

A childish shout jolted Georgie back to the present. She

made admiring noises as her son proudly showed her a small pile of stones he had placed on the patio.

She could remember doing the same thing as a child herself; continuity was important. Her own childhood had been a long way from deprived, but there was a gap—questions that remained unanswered because her mother hadn't been there to answer them. Now Nicky had an absent father… Continuity strikes again!

Her jaw firmed. Rejection wasn't hereditary, it was bad luck, and if she had anything to do with it Nicky was going to be a better judge of character than his mother.

It was strange—she had changed beyond recognition from that girl running away that day on the beach, but the beach house and the town hadn't. It was as if the place were in some sort of time warp.

The town remained defiantly unfashionable. There were no trendy seafood restaurants and no big waves to attract the surfing fraternity, but despite everything Georgie had a soft spot for this place. She rubbed her sandy palms on the seat of her shorts and accepted the seashell Nicky gravely handed her.

This was the first time she'd been back here since that fateful summer. Partly she had come to lay the ghosts of the past and more practically there was no way she could afford a holiday for Nicky any other way.

The jury was still out on whether she had succeeded on the former!

She inhaled, enjoying the salty tang in the air. Memories sort of crept up on you, she reflected. The most unexpected things could trigger them: a smell…texture. As earlier, one second she had been trying to get the sand off her feet before putting on her sandals, the next—*zap*!

It had been incredibly vivid.

Her foot had been in Angolos's lap, his dark head down-bent, gleaming blue-black in the sun as he'd brushed the sand from between her toes. The touch of his fingers had sent delicious little thrills of sensation through her body. He had felt her shiver and his head had lifted. Still holding her eyes, he'd lifted her foot to his mouth and sucked one toe.

Her hand had pressed into the sand as her body had arched. 'You can't do that!' she gasped. Snatching her foot from his grasp, she lifted her knees to her chin.

Angolos's expressive mouth quirked. 'Why?'

'Because you're killing me,' she confessed brokenly.

The way he looked at her, the hungry, predatory gleam in his glittering eyes, made her insides melt. 'You won't have long to wait, *yineka mou*,' he reminded her. 'Tomorrow we will be man and wife.'

Back in the present, Georgie opened her clenched fists. Her palms were damp and inscribed with small half-moons where her neatly trimmed fingernails had dug into the flesh. She sighed and rubbed her palms against the seat of her shorts. Would she ever be able to think about her husband without having a panic attack?

'They could hardly keep their hands off one another.'

The salacious details… This I can *really* do without.

'I'm no prude,' the older woman continued, 'but really…she couldn't keep her hands off him…'

Mortifying though her grandmother's comment was, Georgie, not a person given to self-delusion, had to admit that it was essentially true.

Always a little scornful of her contemporaries' messy and, it seemed to her, painful love affairs, she had been totally unprepared for the primal emotions Angolos had awoken in her. She had been totally mesmerised by him.

'My son and I disagree on most things, but on that occasion we were of one mind. Robert said to her, "Sleep with the man if you must, *live* with him even, but *marry* him…! Insanity."'

'But one we have all experienced, Ann,' came the rueful response.

To imagine the two elderly women experiencing the insanity of blind lust that she had felt with Angolos made Georgie blink.

'The girl has reaped the consequences of her stupidity.'

The scorn in her grandmother's voice brought a flush of mortified colour to Georgie's sun-warmed cheeks. She had made a big mistake and she was willing to own up to it, but she sometimes thought that if her family had their way she would still be eating humble pie when she was eighty!

'She was very young.'

'Young and she thought she knew it all.'

'The young always do. He...the man in the magazine...he looked older?'

'Thirty-two or something like that, I believe, at the time. You have to understand that Georgie was very young for her age...very naïve in many ways, and he had been around the block several times. Oh, a handsome devil, of course. I'm not surprised she fell for him.'

The admission amazed Georgie; to her face her grandmother had never offered any understanding.

'You think he took advantage...?'

'Well, what do you think? A man with one failed marriage to his credit already and Greek.'

From her grandmother's tone it was hard to tell which fault she found harder to forgive in the man: the fact he had been married or the fact he was Greek.

'I knew the moment I saw him he couldn't be trusted. I told her, we *all* told her, but would she listen? No, she *loved* him.'

'Still, you must be proud of the way she has rebuilt her life, and she has a lovely child.'

'A child who has never even seen his father.'

'*Never?* Surely not...?'

'Refused point-blank. Angolos Constantine made it clear that he wanted nothing whatever to do with the child. And neither he or any member of his precious family have ever been near…a blessing, if you ask me.'

It was foolish, but even after this time the truth still had the power to hurt. The knot of pain and anger in Georgie's chest tightened as her glance turned towards the small figure who was crossing the patchy lawn towards her.

His small, sweet face was a mask of concentration as he carried his bucket of pebbles. Her fond gaze followed him as he placed his burden carefully down on the ground and, falling to his chubby knees, began to dig in the soft ground.

The love she felt for her child—the love she had felt for him from the first moment they had laid his warm, slippery little body in her arms—contracted in her chest. She had imagined that magic moment would be shared with Angolos.

How wrong she had been!

She had given birth alone. There had been no husband to hold her hand or breathe through the pain with her, and no one to share the magical moment of birth with.

So Angolos had fallen out of love with her…or more likely he had never been in love with her at all…?

Just why was the question mark attached to that thought, Georgie? A man could not treat anyone he had had any feelings for the way Angolos had treated her.

She had accepted that.

Sure you have!

But how could he reject this child they had produced together? Nicky was perfect… How could anyone not want him? How could any parent *not* love their own child?

'It's just as well that her family were here to pick up the pieces.'

Her grandmother's observation was clearly audible, but Georgie had to strain to hear the other woman's reply. That was the thing about eavesdropping—once you started it was hard to stop.

'That's so sad. How can a man not want to see his child?'

'You tell me. All I know is he hasn't given her a penny and Georgie is too stubborn to ask for what is hers by rights. I told her she should file for divorce and take him for every penny she can. There was no pre-nuptial agreement. I'm afraid Georgie is just like her mother that way—not a practical bone in her body.'

What would Gran say, Georgie wondered, if she knew about the account that Angolos topped up with money every month? Whatever she said she'd say it loudly, especially if she knew that not a penny of the money had been touched!

By now there was a lot of money in that account.

'Mummy…' The tired treble awakened Georgie to the danger of Nicky hearing the conversation taking place in the cottage.

'I'm thirsty.' The small figure, bucket and spade in hand, tugged her shorts.

With a smile, Georgie dropped down to child-level and swept a dark glossy curl from the flushed face of her son. She would never be able to forget what Angolos looked like; she saw his face, or a miniature, childish version of it, every day.

'So am I, darling,' she said, raising her voice to a level that the two elderly women inside could not fail to hear. 'Let's go and see if Granny would like a lemonade too, shall we?'

CHAPTER THREE

ROYALTY was attending the charity performance and the media were out in force to record the event. On the red carpet the star of a soap was denying for the benefit of the TV cameras rumours that she was about to marry her co-star.

The foyer was thronged with other famous faces all wearing their best smiles and designer outfits. Despite the fact all the men present were for the most part similarly dressed in dark, formal suits, Paul had no problem locating the person he had come looking for.

Angolos Constantine stood out in a crowd. It wasn't just his height and looks; it was that rare commodity—*presence*.

'Angolos…?' he called out in relief.

The tall figure, accompanied by an elegant brunette who was dripping with jewels, turned at the sound of his name. A smile spread across his lean face when he identified the speaker.

'Paul!' he exclaimed, detaching his partner from his arm and moving forward, his hand outstretched. 'I didn't know you were an opera buff…'

'I'm not…and even if I was it wouldn't have got me in here,' the shorter man admitted frankly. 'I only got this far by telling them I was your personal physician.'

The groove above Angolos's strong patrician nose deepened. 'That was resourceful of you.' His head whipped slowly from side to side as he searched the crowd. 'And where is the lovely Miranda?'

Paul Radcliff shook his head and scanned the olive-skinned face of the friend he had known since their university days. 'Mirrie's not here.'

24

'I thought you two were joined at the hip.'

'Her blood pressure was up a little...nothing serious,' Paul hastened to assure the other man.

Angolos clapped his hand to his forehead. 'I forgot!' he admitted with a grimace of self-reproach. 'When is my god-child due?'

'Last week.'

Angolos's brows lifted. 'The plot deepens.'

'You're looking well, Angolos.'

It struck him that this was something of an understatement. Nobody looking at the lean, vital figure would have believed that a few years earlier his life had hung in the balance... Paul was one of the few people who did know, and he scarcely believed it himself!

One dark brow slanted sardonically. 'Always the doctor, Paul?' came the soft taunt.

'And friend, I hope.' It was friendship that, after a lot of heart-searching, had brought him here—that and his wife's nagging.

'The man has a right to know, Paul,' she had insisted.

He had still been inclined to leave well alone, but very pregnant wives required humouring. She had insisted that he speak to Angolos without delay and, as she had pointed out, it wasn't the sort of thing you could hit a man with on the phone.

So here he was and he wished he weren't.

The hard features of the darker man softened into a smile of devastating charm. 'And friend,' he agreed quietly. 'So what's wrong, Paul?'

'Nothing's *wrong*, exactly,' Paul returned uncomfortably.

Angolos didn't bother hiding his scepticism. 'Don't give me that. It would take something pretty serious to make you leave Miranda alone just now. It follows that this is serious.'

That was Angolos, logical to his fingertips, except when it

came to his wife. Where Georgie was concerned he got very Greek and unpredictable, reflected the Englishman.

'She…Mirrie, that is, made me come,' Paul admitted.

Angolos nodded. 'And I'm glad she did. I would be insulted if you hadn't come to me with your problem. Just hold on a sec and I'll be with you.'

'*My*…prob…? But *I* haven't got…' Paul stopped and watched with an expression of comical dismay as his friend exchanged words with the brunette, who looked far from happy with what he said. Seconds later Angolos had returned to his side.

'Let's get out of here,' Angolos suggested. 'There's a bar around the corner. We can talk.'

The first thing Paul said when they had ordered their drinks was— 'Let's get one thing straight. I'm not here to touch you for a loan, Angolos.'

'I'm well aware that not all problems can be solved by throwing money at them, Paul.' The level dark-eyed gaze made the other man shift uncomfortably. 'But if yours ever can be I will throw money at them whether you like it or not.' The hauteur in his strong-boned face was replaced by a warm smile as he added, 'My friend, if it wasn't for you I wouldn't be here at all.'

'Nonsense.'

The other man's patent discomfort made Angolos grin, his teeth flashing white in the darkness of his face. 'Your British self-deprecation borders on the ludicrous, Paul,' he observed wryly. He set his elbows on the table and leant forward, his expression attentive. 'Now what's the problem?'

'I wouldn't call it a problem… It's just that Dr Monroe retired and his patients have been relocated to us…' In response to Angolos's frown Paul breathed in deeply and went on quickly. 'Yesterday my partner was called out on an emergency and I saw some of the new patients.' He swallowed. 'Georgie…your Georgie was one of them.'

Angolos's expression didn't change, but his actions as he picked up his untouched drink and lifted it to his lips were strangely deliberate. A moment later, having replaced the glass on the table, he lifted his eyes to those of the other man.

'Is she ill?'

'No, no!'

Almost imperceptibly Angolos's shoulders relaxed.

He privately acknowledged that it was slightly perverse, considering he had cursed his faithless wife with all the inventive and vindictive power at his disposal three and a half years earlier, that the possibility of her being ill now should have awoken such primitive protective instincts.

'Actually she looked fantastic…a bit thin, perhaps,' Paul conceded half to himself. 'She always had great bones.'

'I have not the faintest interest in how she looks.' Angolos's jaw tightened as the other man turned an overtly sceptical gaze on his face. 'And I don't remember you mentioning her great bones when you told me I would be making the greatest mistake of my life if I married her…'

'Ah, well, I was afraid that you were…'

'Out of my mind?' Angolos suggested when his friend stumbled. 'You were right on both counts, as it happened.' Elbows set on the table, he leaned forward slightly. 'Did she ask you to intercede on my behalf? I thought you had more sense than to be taken in by—'

The doctor looked indignant. 'Actually, mate, I got the distinct impression you're the last person she wants to contact,' he revealed frankly.

'Indeed!'

'She was pretty shocked when she saw me. In fact,' he admitted, 'I thought she was going to run out of the office. And when I said your name she looked…' He stopped; there were no words that could accurately describe the bleak expression that had filled the young mother's eyes. 'Not happy,' Paul finished lamely.

Angolos leaned back in his seat and, loosening a button on his jacket, folded his arms across his chest. 'Yet you are here.'

'I am.' Paul ran a hand across his jaw. 'This is hard. Mirrie does this sort of thing so much better than I do.'

At this point, if he had been having this conversation with anyone else Angolos would have told them to get on with it, but this was Paul, so he controlled his impatience and made suitably encouraging noises.

'The thing is, Angolos, she brought the boy.' The expression on his friend's face as he looked at him from beneath knitted brows was less than encouraging, but Paul persisted. 'Have you ever seen…?'

'No, I have never seen the child,' Angolos responded glacially.

'He's a fine little lad and not spoilt either. Georgie's done a fine job, though I got the impression reading between the lines that money's tight.'

Angolos's lip curled contemptuously. 'So this is what this is about—she's been playing the poverty card. I deposit a more than adequate amount of money in a bank account for the child's needs. If Georgette has got greedy, if she has some deluded hope of extracting a more substantial amount from me, she can forget it. She's taken me for a fool once…'

'She honestly didn't mention money, Angolos, but if she wanted to bleed you… Did you see how much that rock star who denied paternity got taken for when the girl took him to court? DNA testing can—'

'DNA testing,' Angolos cut in, 'has robbed her of the opportunity of passing the child off as mine. If she's that desperate she could always sell her story to some tabloid.' His nostrils flared as he drummed his long fingers on the tabletop. 'That would be her style.'

'Wouldn't she have done that before now if she was going

to? And if she wanted money I imagine the divorce settlement would be pretty generous.'

'Over my dead body.'

'I get the feeling you mean that literally.'

'I was hoping it wouldn't come to that,' Angolos returned smoothly. 'Are we drifting here, Paul?'

'Yes, well, actually, it's…the DNA thing…'

'The DNA thing?' Angolos said blankly.

'Are you totally sure a test would come up *negative*?'

'Sure…?' Angolos looked at his friend incredulously. 'You of all people can ask me that? The chemo saved my life but there was a price to pay—it rendered me sterile. My only chance of having a child is stored in a deep-freeze somewhere.'

'It was tough luck,' Paul, very conscious of his own impending fatherhood, admitted.

'*Tough luck?*' Angolos's expressive mouth dropped at one corner. 'Yes, I suppose it was tough luck. However, considering that without the treatment and, more importantly, your early diagnosis I would not be here at all, I consider myself lucky.'

'But it's not an easy thing to come to terms with.'

'Actually, *intellectually* I have no problem with the situation, but somehow, no matter how many times I tell myself there's more to a man's masculinity than his sperm count, I still feel…' His mouth twisted in a self-derisive smile, he met Paul's eyes. 'Maybe Georgette was right about that, at least—perhaps at heart I am an unreconstructed chauvinist…'

'Was there ever any doubt?'

This retort drew a rueful smile from Angolos.

'Is that why you never told her about the chemo and the cancer? Were you afraid she'd…?' Paul gave an embarrassed grimace. 'Sorry, I shouldn't…'

'Was I afraid she'd think me any less a man, you mean? What do you think, Paul?'

'I think if I knew what went on in your head I'd be the only one,' his friend returned frankly. 'You know, when it comes to answering questions you'd give the slipperiest politician a run for his money. If you want my opinion, you were wrong. I know Georgie was young, but she always struck me as pretty mature…'

'Mature enough to cheat on me and try to pass off the product of her amorous adventures as mine.'

Paul winced. 'Ah, about that, Angolos…'

'You want to discuss my wife's infidelity?'

'Of course not.'

'If you've discovered who her lover was…' Right up to the end she had refused to admit her guilt or provide the name of her lover. Though he knew who he was. 'I'm really no longer interested.'

'Maybe there was no lover?'

Angolos's dark brows knitted as he gave a contemptuous smile. 'Was no lover…? What are you suggesting—immaculate conception?'

Paul held up his hand. 'Angolos, hear me out. I know that the sort of chemotherapy you had normally results in infertility, but there are exceptions…you didn't have any tests post—'

'No, or the counselling, which apparently would have made me content to be less than a man.'

'Yes, you made your opinion of counselling quite plain at the time.'

'One cannot alter what has happened; one must just accept.'

'Terribly fatalistic and fine.'

'We Greeks are fatalists.'

'You're the least fatalistic person I've ever met. And sometimes it helps to talk…but I didn't come here to discuss the benefits of counselling.'

'Are you likely to tell me what you did come for any time this side of Christmas?'

'The boy is yours.'

A spasm of anger passed across Angolos's face. Paul watched with some trepidation as his friend took several deep breaths. There was a white line etched around his lips as he said in a low, carefully controlled voice, 'Anyone but you…Paul…'

'You'd knock my block off, I know, but I still have to say it. The boy, Angolos, he's the living spit of you. Oh, I don't mean a little bit like—I mean a miniature version. There's absolutely no doubt about it in my mind—Nicky is your son.'

'Is this some sort of joke, Paul?'

'I've got a warped sense of humour, Angolos, but I'm not cruel. If you don't believe me I suggest you go look for yourself.'

'I'm not buying into this fantasy.'

'They're staying at the beach place.'

'I have absolutely no intention of going anywhere near that woman.'

'Well, that's up to you, but if it was me—'

Angolos's eyes flashed. 'It is not you. You have a wife waiting for you at home; you will hold your newly born child in your arms…' He saw the shock on the other man's face and, worse, the dawning sympathy. 'The truth is, Paul,' Angolos added in a more moderate tone, 'I envy you. Never take what you have for granted.'

CHAPTER FOUR

PEOPLE sitting in the hotel sun lounge opposite, munching their cream teas, watched as the tall, dark-haired figure emerged from the Mercedes convertible and adjusted his designer shades. A buzz of speculation passed through the room.

Who was the stranger? There was a general consensus that he looked as though he was *somebody*.

It was exactly as he remembered it, Angolos decided as he scanned the beach. Progress and the twenty-first century had still to reach this backwater.

Despite the fact the sun had retreated behind some sinister-looking dark clouds, there was still a sprinkling of hardy, inadequately clad individuals on the sands. Some were even in the water, which, if his memory served him correctly, was cold enough to freeze a man, especially one accustomed to the warmth of the Aegean, to the core.

Angolos had no specific plan of action. He knew that Paul was wrong; he had made this journey simply to extinguish any lingering doubts. After all, the unformed features of one dark-eyed, dark-haired child looked very much like another.

Saying the resemblance was striking was hardly proof positive. Frankly the unscientific approach from someone who really ought to know better surprised him.

Paul had to be wrong.

Then why are you here?

Because, he admitted to the dry voice in his head, if I don't see this child for myself I'll never know for sure. A niggling doubt—or was it hope?—would always be there. Irrational, of course; if he had a son he would *know*. It was simply not possible.

32

The part of the sea front he had reached was newly pedestrianised. There were signs excluding litter, dogs, and skateboards…and it had worked; he had the stretch pretty much to himself. He could see the church spire in the distance. He knew if he headed in that general direction he would end up where he wanted to be.

Although in these circumstances *want* was not really an appropriate term.

The Kemps' holiday home was reached by a narrow, tree-lined lane that ran one side of the churchyard. A more direct route was via the beach—the house boasted a garden gate that gave direct access to the dunes and sand.

Angolos chose the more direct route. The sooner this nonsense was over with, the better, as far as he was concerned. He could not really spare the time as it was.

Angolos was not a man who lived in the past, but under the circumstances it was hard to prevent his thoughts returning to the first occasion he had walked along this stretch of sand.

He had been euphoric after receiving the final all-clear from the hospital earlier that morning. His first thought had been to immediately drive down to the coast to share the good news with the friend whom he owed his life to. If Paul hadn't picked up on those few tell-tale symptoms and cajoled him into having a blood test that had revealed his problem, he'd had no doubt that he would not have been here now.

His plans had been frustrated. Paul and his wife Miranda hadn't been at home. Driving along the sea-front road on his way back to the capital, on impulse Angolos had pulled the car over.

The sea air had filled his nostrils; the sun had warmed his face; he had felt alive…he had been alive.

There was nothing like a brush with death to make a man appreciate things he would normally have overlooked, but even had his senses not been heightened he would have noticed her. Why one pretty girl should have attracted his attention when there were so many pretty girls in the world remained a mystery.

Maybe it was the fact she had refused his impulsive offer of dinner that had made the honey-haired English girl with the golden eyes remain in his mind the rest of the day.

And maybe it had been coincidence that had made him return to the beach late that evening when the light had been fading, but Angolos was more inclined to consider it fate.

And fate was not always kind.

When he'd tried the second time, Paul and Mirrie had been home. They had opened a bottle of champagne to celebrate and had insisted he should stay the night. He ought to have been able to relax—he had been given his life back; he had been in the company of friends—but Angolos had felt strangely restless.

The evening had been sticky and stifling; a few distant rumbles had promised thunder. When he'd announced his intention of taking a walk on the beach, his understanding hosts had said fine, and given him a key to let himself in.

Walking along the pebbly foreshore, he hadn't immediately appreciated that the figure in the waves had been in trouble. Assuming the swimmer had been messing around or drunk, he had turned a deaf ear to the cries.

When he had realised what had been happening he had responded instinctively to the situation. On autopilot he had fought his way out of his jacket as he'd run down the beach, pausing only at the water's edge to step out of his shoes.

He was a strong swimmer and, even hampered by his clothing, it had taken him very little time to cover the hundred or so metres. Even though clearly exhausted, desperation had lent the struggling swimmer strength as she had wrapped her arms around his neck, dragging him down. She had clung like a limpet—yes, even in the desperation of trying to break her stranglehold, he had registered that the body sealed to his was female—and in his weakened condition it had taken him a few worrying minutes to subdue her.

Fortunately she had appeared to have exhausted herself fighting him, and had remained passive as he'd towed her to shore. The undercurrent, which had presumably been too strong for her to negotiate, had been against him on the way back. The swim back had taken its toll on his remaining strength.

The relief when he'd got her ashore had been intense.

It wasn't until he had carried the limp and bedraggled figure from the water and dumped her, coughing, onto the sand that he had recognised her. Lying at his feet had been the golden-eyed girl from earlier.

Something had snapped in his head. That someone like this girl with everything to look forward to could have been so careless of life when he'd known how fragile and precious it was had incensed him beyond measure.

Anger had coursed through his body and brain, causing his vision to blur and his hands to shake. He hadn't been able to recall being this angry in his life—not even when the doctors had given him a poor prognosis. On that occasion he had had to control his feelings, but not now. He had been incandescent with rage.

Dropping down onto his knees beside her, he had taken her small heart-shaped face between his hands, pushing aside the drenched strands of hair that had clung like fronds of exotic seaweed to her face.

He had been able to feel the rapid beat of the pulse that had throbbed in her blue-veined temple. Her taut breasts had lifted as she'd tried to drag air into her oxygen-starved lungs. The black swimsuit had clung to her supple young body as lovingly as a second skin. Her skin, he'd noticed, had an incredible, luminescent clarity, at that moment it had been icy cold.

The image of her lying there was so perfect it might have

happened yesterday. His body responded to the memory as if it had been that night nearly four years earlier. He was rock-hard.

'How could you be so stupid?' he demanded then. He shook her until her eyes opened.

Amazing amber eyes, big and not quite focused, blinked back at him. She was exhibiting classic signs of shock, but he was in no mood to make allowances.

'I didn't think…I…I mean it was—'

'Did you want to kill yourself?' he ranted on, oblivious to her pitiful and barely audible apology.

'Of c…course not.'

'You could have drowned us both.' Her eyes widened; the swimming depths reflected mute horror. 'What the hell were you doing?'

'I was swimming.'

'No, you were bloody drowning!' He watched her full lower lip tremble and without thinking covered her mouth with his own.

Even now, all this time later, he could recall her startled gasp, the salty taste of the soft lips that parted sweetly under his and the softness of her body as she went bonelessly limp. The deep, soundless shudder that sighed through her body would stay with him for ever.

From somewhere he dredged up the strength to lift his mouth from hers when all he wanted to do was explore the sweet, moist recesses. Her fierce little groan of protest as the contact was broken made him forget for several dangerous seconds why this wasn't a good idea.

The tenacious fingers that curled tightly in his wet hair proved infinitely more difficult to resist than the tide that had tried to pull them under.

He grabbed her hands and pinned them above her head, just to stop her touching him. 'You don't want to do this.'

'You're insane,' she contended, shaking.

'Certifiable,' Angolos agreed thickly. The slim body beneath his was burning up. He could feel the blast of heat through the layers of wet clothes that separated them.

'Don't stop!' The husky command wreaked havoc with his already-shredded self-control. She was like fire in his arms, supple, soft and displaying the same sort of savage desperation that thundered through his veins.

He hadn't held a woman for almost a year, let alone had sex.

When he had first been diagnosed, his life had been thrown into utter confusion. He had always known where he was going and how he was getting there. The only restrictions placed on him had been by the responsibilities that had come with the privilege attached to his birth.

His focus and self-belief had always been enough to get him where he wanted to be. Helplessness had never entered the picture; then he had lost control. Someone had moved the goalposts and he had been angry.

He hadn't realised how angry until he had said to the consultant treating him, 'Tell me straight, Doctor, could this thing kill me?'

'Yes, Mr Constantine, it could, but not if I have anything to do with it.'

It was a week later that he had woken up next to a woman, and he hadn't known her name.

It had been a wake-up call. He had never ducked a fight in his life, but that, he'd then realised, was what he had been doing.

He had never been a saint, but he had always been discriminating and one-night stands had never been on his agenda. He had told himself to stop wallowing in self-pity, and had cleaned up his act. Of course later, when the treatment had taken his body to the limits of endurance, escaping into mindless sex had not been an option. He hadn't had the strength, let alone the inclination.

That evening on the beach had been the first time in months that he had felt the stirring of sex…finding the object of his fantasy in his arms, half naked and begging him to kiss her, had transformed those stirrings into a raw, raging hunger.

He must have retained a shred of sanity because he had tried to stop, he could remember loosing her wrists and putting out a hand to lift himself off her, but instead his fingers had closed over the soft curve of one small, perfect breast.

The air had suddenly vibrated with the sexual tension that had erupted between them. Angolos had been immobilised by a wave of lust. In his head he had seen himself pushing aside the black material to reveal the straining pink bud. He had seen himself run his tongue over the straining peak, had heard her soft moan of pleasure…no, the soft moan had been real.

'That feels so…' Mesmerised, he watched her lips form a soundless *oh* as, eyes closed tight, her body arched.

'I want you.'

Her eyes flicked open, tawny and wild. The most beautiful eyes he had ever seen. 'I'm yours.' She reached up and slid her hands under his wet shorts, letting her fingers slide over his skin.

Of course he lost it; what man wouldn't? He pulled her under him and traced the shape of her skull with his fingers, lifting the heavy wet hair from the nape of her lovely neck. The sound that vibrated in her throat as her head fell back reminded him of a cat's purr.

Her eyes opened and he touched his finger to the corner of her wide mouth and traced the full, soft outline. 'You have the most amazing lips,' he told her thickly. 'And such beautiful, beautiful eyes…tiger's eyes.'

'You're amazing all over.'

He allowed himself to kiss her then, driving his tongue into her mouth. He felt her searching hands on his body, sliding beneath his steaming clothes, baring his flesh to the air.

As his body pressed her into the wet sand she was still

shaking and so was he, no longer with cold or anger, but with a wild, frenzied desire. Through the wet clothes separating them he felt the fresh wave of sexual heat that washed over her skin. She wrapped her legs around him and gasped as she felt his erection press into her soft belly.

Angolos wanted to bury himself in that softness more than he wanted to take another breath. He might have done just that, if the night hadn't suddenly been illuminated by a jagged shaft of lightning. Lightning so bright he could see it through his closed eyelids.

He rolled off her with a groan and as he lay there panting there was a roll of thunder that broke directly overhead. The rain began to fall then, cold on his overheated skin.

She touched his shoulder and he shook his head. 'I am not in control,' he told her thickly.

'Me neither. Good, isn't it…?' She sighed. 'You don't have to worry. I'm not afraid of thunder, and the boyfriend…I was lying. I don't really have one. And I don't expect…'

He turned his head. 'You don't expect what?'

'I don't expect it to be…you know…the first time…'

The husky confidence made him freeze. '*Theos!* Can it be true…?' He scanned her face and knew. 'Dear God, it is.'

A man who prided himself on his control, he couldn't believe what he had just done. If it hadn't been for the storm he…

She reached for him and she looked hurt when he jerked back avoiding contact.

He had never wanted a woman so much in his life.

'You're mad with me…?'

He looked at the tears trembling on her eyelashes and cursed slowly and fluently under his breath.

'No, I'm mad with me,' he told her as he picked her up.

She lay passively in his arms as he carried her across the sand dunes to where his car was parked in a quiet lane. The place was totally deserted as he dumped her in the front seat.

'Are you kidnapping me?' There was no alarm in her voice, just a lazy curiosity.

'No, I'm warming you up,' he said, switching on the engine and turning up the heater full blast.

'Maybe I should take off my wet things…?'

The only wet thing she was wearing was a black swimsuit with a zip up the front. 'Maybe you shouldn't,' he said, trying hard not to think about that strategically placed zip. *One tug…*

'I don't think I should have got in a car with a stranger,' she observed absently as he draped a jacket that had been in the back seat over her shoulders.

'You didn't get in. I put you in.'

'So you did. I'm warmer.' She leaned back in the deeply upholstered seat with a sigh. 'You know, I don't think I'm quite myself,' she confided.

That makes two of us. 'You nearly drowned.'

Her eyes, which had been closing, suddenly flickered open. Tawny eyes scanned his face. 'You kissed me.' She pressed a hand to her soft lips. 'I liked it.'

Beside her he didn't dare move; he didn't trust himself to speak. The ferocious tension in his body was so extreme that he remembered the bones in his face aching.

'I noticed,' he admitted.

She lifted a hand and ran a finger down his lean cheek. 'Are you going to do it again?'

'You're in shock.'

'I'm something, but not that. I think you saved my life. How can I repay you?'

He caught hold of her wrist and dragged her hand from his face. 'Well, you can cut that out, for a start.'

She flinched visibly at the cutting response. After a second's hurt incomprehension, a tide of mortified colour washed over her face.

'*Theos!* Don't look at me like that,' he pleaded throatily.

She bit her lip and fixed her eyes on her hands, which lay clenched in her lap.

'I'm s…sorry,' she stuttered. 'I really don't know what came over me.'

'The same thing that came over me. Where do you live? I'll take you home.' And after that he was going to drive away in the opposite direction.

He didn't do virgins.

CHAPTER FIVE

'CAN we have the ball back, mister?'

The request dragged Angolos back from a time he mostly succeeded in blanking from his mind.

To his way of thinking, no useful purpose could be served from preserving the memory of a time when he had allowed himself to be humiliated and deceived, except possibly to learn a lesson. He would never trust a woman again.

Had it amused Georgette to see him oblivious to her affair? Had she laughed with her lover as they had planned to pass the child off as his…?

A muscle clenched in Angolos's lean cheek as he pulled a hand across his brow to wipe off the moisture that clung to his tanned skin. It had started raining and he hadn't noticed; neither had he noticed until now that he was within a hundred yards of the gate that led to the garden of the Kemp house, a slightly battered timber cottage with a tin roof. Bending, he picked up the ball that lay at his feet and threw it back to the family playing a game of beach cricket.

'Good throw,' somebody acknowledged cheerily before they returned to their game.

Angolos headed for the gate. It creaked on the rusty hinges as he pushed it open. His lips curled in distaste as his hand rested on the peeling paintwork. At one time he had found the shabby chic of the Kemp home, so totally unlike what he was accustomed to, charming. Now he just found it, well… shabby.

The family he had never found charming and the feeling was mutual. Her relatives had come across as a bunch of xenophobic idiots who had been appalled at the idea of one of their number marrying a foreigner. Later, when Georgette had confided that her mother had run off with a Greek waiter, her family's attitude had been more understandable.

His critical glance skimmed the semi-screened area. The cottage and garden looked the same as he remembered; the only thing that hadn't been here four years ago was the clutter of children's toys. Angolos's dark eyes were drawn against his will to the evidence of childish occupation…the tricycle, the plastic toy cars, the bucket of shells gathered from the beach.

His classical profile tautened as he averted his gaze and strode purposefully to the door. There was absolutely no point prolonging this.

The door was opened before he had an opportunity to announce his arrival. His raised hand fell to his side as he looked at the woman framed in the open doorway. She was, he judged, somewhere in her mid-fifties, her grey-streaked dark hair was cut in a short modern crop, she had intelligent blue eyes and an interesting rather than attractive face.

She was a stranger to Angolos.

'Hello, I'm—'

'Good gracious, you're Nicky's father.'

Angolos was so surprised by her automatic assumption that his response was uncharacteristically unguarded. 'No, I'm not anyone's father,' he ejaculated bitterly.

'Nonsense, of course you are,' she dismissed, dealing him an amused look.

Angolos was taken aback by this response. 'I will not argue the point with you.'

The woman scanned his face, then threw back her head and laughed, not intimidated by the hauteur in his manner.

Angolos liked that.

In his position there were too many people ready to say what he wanted to hear. They had been saying what he wanted to hear since the day he'd stepped into his dead father's shoes at the age of twenty-two. He valued people who could look him in the eyes and say, 'You're wrong.'

'Well, that would be rather pointless, wouldn't it?'

'It would?'

'Most definitely,' came the robust response. 'You want to see Nicky…of course you do,' she added before he had an opportunity to respond. 'May I be frank?'

'Can I stop you?' he wondered.

The dry intonation brought a fleeting smile to the woman's lips. 'This puts me in an awkward position…' she confided. 'I have no idea what agreement you have…visiting rights and so forth? Actually I didn't think you saw him at all.' She studied the tall man's face. 'I can see you don't want to discuss your personal business with a nosy old woman.'

'I can assure you I have not come to kidnap the boy.'

'I'm glad to hear it, but under the circumstances it might be better if you came back when Georgie is home.'

'But the child is here?' Angolos probed and saw the older woman's expression become guarded. 'The thing is, Mrs…?'

'My name is Ruth Simmons. *Miss.*'

'Miss Simmons, I'm rather pushed for time.'

The woman eyed him with patent disapproval. 'After all these years?'

Angolos supposed he ought to have expected this. Georgette had obviously decided to paint herself as the injured party and him as the unnatural father. His broad shoulders lifted in an infinitesimal shrug. Did she plan to poison this child's mind in a similar manner…poor kid?

'When do you expect Georgette to return?'

Ruth Simmons looked uncertainly at the remote and quite sensationally handsome face of Nicky's father and her brow puckered.

'I really couldn't say.' Was this the sort of man who would turn his back on his own child? He didn't seem the type…

Of course, you could never tell, but the Greeks she had met were very family orientated.

'Couldn't or won't…?' He lifted one long-fingered hand in an unconsciously elegant gesture. 'No matter.' He consulted his watch. 'I will return at a more convenient moment.' And then again maybe I won't… After all, the entire exercise was totally pointless. Better to get in his car and drive back to London.

The tall man's mechanical smile did not reach his eyes; Ruth noticed all the same that it was effortlessly charming. In the flesh this man was even more startlingly good-looking. If I were twenty years younger…? The self-mocking smile that curved her lips vanished as a loud bang followed by an even louder wail emerged from the living room.

'What now?' she cried, hurrying inside.

Angolos stepped through the open door.

A few moments later, with the crying child cradled in her arms, Ruth viewed the damage. It could have been worse. Still, it was a pity that her friend was fond of the hideous ornate Victorian bust that was now lying in fragments on the floor. The overturned chair was a clue as to how the three-year-old had managed to reach the shelf where it had been displayed.

'Did you fall, Nicky?' Her matter-of-fact tone and manner had a soothing effect upon the crying child, who stopped to catch his breath. 'Poor you,' she said, rubbing the obvious bruise that was developing on the child's forehead. 'Did you hurt yourself anywhere else, sweetheart?'

Nicky shook his head. 'Granny will be cross…'

'No, I'm sure she won't.'

'She will,' the child, whose tears had subsided, retorted positively. 'Who are you?' he asked, poking a chubby hand in the direction of the stranger.

'Gracious!' Ruth exclaimed, realising for the first time that the tall Greek had followed her into the room. He was standing there frozen. The only flicker of movement in his body was supplied by his stunning eyes, which were trained on the child in her arms.

Without replying, he continued to draw air into his lungs through clenched teeth, like a man who had forgotten how to breathe. As he squatted, bringing his face level with the toddler, she saw that his gloriously golden skin had acquired a greyish tinge. She saw his lips move; nothing came out.

'Gracious!' she added once more and with feeling. The physical similarity between father and son was truly startling... Nicky began to cry again.

'Nicky...your name is Nicky?' The tearful boy nodded his head.

Georgie walked in through the open door weighed down by supermarket carrier bags filled with groceries. A car, she reflected wistfully, would make life a lot easier, but her budget didn't run to such luxuries.

'Big boys don't cry, Nicky.'

She froze, the blood draining from her face. It was a voice Georgie would never, *could* never, forget.

It was a voice she heard in her dreams and her nightmares.

She stood there oblivious to the eggs that had broken when she'd dropped her bags and were now running stickily over the carpet.

This isn't happening.

Her first instinct was to run as fast and as far away as possible. She subdued her selfish reflex...she couldn't run and leave Nicky. Anyway, running would have been futile if Angolos wanted her. A shudder slid down her spine. When Angolos wanted something he was totally focused and implacable.

Only Angolos didn't want her; he had made that perfectly clear.

Her heart was hammering in her chest and her feet felt as

though they had lead weights attached as she moved towards the living-room door. Her head was spinning but one question amongst the many that chased one another around in her mind was uppermost.

Why had Angolos turned up now?

'I'm not a big boy. I'm lit…ul. Go away!'

Georgie heard the childish treble and her shoulders straightened. Leave him alone, she wanted to yell as she rushed impetuously forward.

She might prefer to walk into a lion's den than voluntarily enter a room that held her husband, but, as she had learnt within two seconds of his birth, for Nicky she would do the unthinkable. Her own needs and desires would always be secondary to her son's best interests…it was being a mother.

As she stepped through the door she almost collided with Ruth, who had offered to look after Nicky while she caught the last post and picked up some groceries and while her mother was staying with Robert. The woman barely seemed to register her presence.

Georgie's eyes moved past her and gasped. Having enough volts to light up a county pass through her body could not have felt more shocking than looking at father and son.

'Oh, my!' she whispered. *His hair still curled on his neck the same way.*

She had never denied to herself the startling resemblance between Nicky and his father but now seeing them side by side it was impossible for anyone to ignore. The sight of the long, lean figure balanced on his heels in front of the child wiped every thought from her head… She felt desire clutch low in her belly.

She grimaced in self-disgust. It appalled her and, yes, *scared* her that, even after all this time and everything he had done to her, she still only had to look at him to be reduced to a screaming mass of hormones.

Georgie took a deep sustaining breath and lifted her chin. 'Come here, Nicky,' she said quietly.

She was aware that Angolos's attention had slewed towards her. The hand she stretched towards her son had a perceptible tremor, but she studiously ignored him and kept her eyes trained on Nicky's tear-stained face.

It was only a moment before the child responded, but during that moment she had to fight back the impulse that urged her to rush over and physically tear him away from the man whose hands lay on his shoulders. Her clenched hands relaxed as Nicky aimed himself at her like a small but determined heat-seeking missile.

Angolos rose to his feet in time to see Georgie bend forward, her softly waving hair spilling across her face. She pushed the silky hank impatiently behind her ear.

'What have you been doing, darling?' Her attention on the child, Georgie didn't see the spasm of something close to pain that contorted her estranged husband's dark, autocratic features as he watched them.

'He had a slight accident. It was my fault...I only left him for a moment,' Ruth interjected.

'With Nicky a moment is all it takes,' Georgie responded as she hugged her son to her. 'Isn't it, champ?' she said, brushing the curly dark hair from his brow as she straightened up with the child's body pressed close to her own. She saw the bruise and sighed. 'In the wars, I see.'

She knew that pretending Angolos wasn't there wasn't exactly a long-term solution to her present predicament, but it was the only one she could think of. Angolos, all six feet four of him, was there barely a metre away from her, looking even more devastatingly attractive than she remembered... Her brain just refused to deal with the reality of the situation.

The muscles in her face ached as she forced a tense smile. 'Now, why don't you go with Auntie Ruth?' She caught the eye of the older woman, who gave an understanding grimace.

'I'm really sorry about this, Georgie.' Her soft apology was accompanied by a sideways look towards the tall man who was silently watching.

'It's not your fault,' Georgie said, handing over her burden. 'This will only take a minute,' she promised, staying one step ahead of her rising panic by sheer force of will alone.

A silent sigh of relief passed through her body as they left the room.

'Do you always reward him for misbehaving?' Angolos's eyes were flat and icy as they scanned her face.

Georgie waited until she judged the child was out of earshot before responding and opened her eyes. 'What would you do—beat him?'

Her sneering suggestion made his face tauten with anger. 'Children need to know what the boundaries are. It makes them feel secure.'

'Hearing you throw around terms like security in connection with Nicky...' She swallowed back the anger that made her want to scream at him and hammer her fists against his chest. Her voice dropped to a low, scornful whisper. 'You lost any right you might have had to criticise the way I bring up *my* child when you effectively disowned him.'

Angolos's head reared as though she had struck him. 'I would never knowingly disown my son.' His low, uneven voice throbbed with sincerity. His mesmeric eyes locked onto hers.

'I stand corrected. You *accidentally* disowned him, which makes it all right, then.' She went to the door and yanked it open. 'You were just passing, I suppose, so feel free to carry on doing just that.'

'You want me to leave?'

Georgie, her expression stony, fixed her eyes on the wall directly ahead. 'The only thing I want more is for you to be kidnapped by aliens, but I'm realistic, I'll settle for the former.'

He dragged his long fingers through his hair. The sheer familiarity of the gesture made her ache.

'We need to talk.'

She turned her head; he was incredible…really incredible! Did he really think she was going to let him waltz in here and mess up her life for a second time?

'Did I really ever find your autocratic mannerisms a turn-on?'

She hadn't realised until he responded in a dry tone that she had voiced her thoughts out loud. 'I don't know, did you?'

Subduing a mortified blush, she gave an indifferent shrug. '*I* don't need to talk,' she told him stonily.

'Then listen.'

Georgie closed her eyes and stuffed her fingers in her ears. Through clenched teeth she began to hum loudly and tunelessly.

'You still haven't grown up, then.'

Georgie's blazing eyes lifted to the contemptuous face of the man who had captured her wrists. '*Me? I'm* not the one who throws away a relationship as casually as a spoilt brat throws away a toy that he's got tired of.'

His breath whistled in a startled gasp through his clenched teeth. 'What did you say?'

'It roughly translates as get the hell out of here and my life… *I hate and despise you!*' She twisted her hands angrily, but instead of releasing her Angolos jerked her towards him.

The breath whooshed out of her lungs as her body collided with a body that had no give. For one shocked moment she stood there feeling the strong, steady thud of his heart, then she began to struggle. She fought the rising tide of sensual inertia so powerful that it threatened to swamp her as much as the strong hands that imprisoned her. She fought because deep down there was a secret part of her that didn't want to escape, a part of her that wanted to melt into him.

'Let me go… How dare…?'

Suddenly she was free.

The brief skirmish had only lasted a matter of seconds, but Georgie was fighting for breath as though she'd just gone five rounds with a contender for the title.

Rubbing one wrist, she glared at him. Angolos had always been lean and hard in a tensile steel sort of way, he still didn't carry an ounce of spare flesh, but that brief contact had revealed that he had bulked out muscle-wise. The treacherous burst of heat low in her belly filled her with intense shame.

'I'd like you to leave,' she told him huskily.

'When I've said what I came to say.'

Georgie gave a frustrated little grunt... Well, that much hadn't changed; Angolos was still as stubborn and incapable of compromise as ever. 'Get your lawyer to write mine a letter,' she suggested. 'Isn't that the way it usually works?'

'You don't have a lawyer...'

'And you don't have a chance in hell of getting me to listen to you.'

He studied her set, stubborn face and stony eyes for a moment before dragging a hand through his already disordered thick dark hair.

'I need a drink.'

'There's a pub around the corner. They're not fussy about who they serve.'

His eyes narrowed. 'The Kemp household still represents the best of British hospitality, I see.'

Georgie hardly heard him; the muscle that clenched and unclenched in his cheek was having a strongly hypnotic effect on her. Dressed all in black, he looked sleek and dangerous and off-the-scale sexy!

'The house and town are the same, but you,' he added, allowing his frowning gaze to move over her slender figure, 'look different...'

Careful not to reveal by so much of a flicker of an eyelash what the critical brush of his eyes did to her, Georgie shrugged and stuck her hands in the pockets of her jeans. She was oblivious to the fact the action stretched the material, lovingly revealing the feminine curve of her slim thighs.

'Designer clothes, you mean?' She gave a contemptuous smile. 'They don't suit my lifestyle and actually they're not me. They never were.'

When Angolos lifted his eyes to her face his natural warm colouring was a shade deeper. 'Actually I meant you look *harder*.' Despite this grim assertion, it was her *softness* that was occupying his thoughts.

You carry on believing that, thought Georgie, pushing her hands deeper into her pockets to disguise the fact they were seriously trembling.

'There was a time when I actually cared what you thought of me...' The memory of her anxiety to please him made her shake her head in pained distaste.

The irony was, the harder she tried to be what he wanted, the farther apart they seemed to drift. All the expensive clothes in the world had not made her fit in with the wealthy, snooty Constantine clan.

From day one his family, or more specifically his mother, Olympia Constantine, had made no attempt to hide her disapproval...at least not from Georgie. Around Angolos his mother had been more circumspect. Olympia had saved her sly digs and outright hostility for when Angolos hadn't been around, which had been most of the time. She had never made any secret of the fact she'd wanted Georgie out of their lives.

And in the end they had got what they'd wanted. Georgie released her breath in a long, shuddering sigh and lifted her chin.

'I'm not the pushover I once was, certainly.' She was faintly amazed to hear her voice emerge steady and even. 'I don't know why you're here, Angolos, and I don't want to know.' She stood to one side and gestured to the open door.

Angolos didn't move. A muscle along his strong jaw spasmed as he picked up a toy car from the floor. She watched warily as he pushed the toy back and forth along across his palm. 'He's my son.'

Georgie's slender shoulders lifted. *'So…?'*

He dropped the toy into an overflowing toy box and lifted a hand to his forehead, rubbing the groove between his dark brows. He continued to look uncharacteristically distracted. *'I have a son.'*

'You say it as if it's news, Angolos,' she mocked. 'You've had a son for the past three years and I didn't notice you breaking any speed records to see him. Not even a b…birthday card.' She lowered her eyes quickly as she felt the warmth of the unshed tears that filled them.

'I thought my lawyers made it clear that if the money I deposited wasn't sufficient I would—'

Georgie's head came up, her luminous, liquid golden eyes levelled contemptuously with his. 'Do you really think I'd touch a penny of your money…?'

Angolos's lip curled. 'You expect me to believe that you haven't touched the money.'

'I never wanted your money!' she flared. 'I wanted…' She stopped dead, dark colour suffusing her pale cheeks. 'If I gave a damn what you believe I'd get out the bank statement.' She had given a damn once, though, and it had hurt her more than she wanted to remember.

'If you haven't used the money, how have you supported yourself?' he demanded suspiciously. 'Or should I ask *who* has been supporting you?'

She sucked in an outraged breath through flared nostrils and watched the toy ball he had aimed a kick at bounce off the wall.

If he thought she had time for a social life, let alone a boyfriend, he really didn't have the first clue about what it took to bring up a child single-handed while holding down a demanding job! But then maybe that was all to the good—she preferred the idea of him thinking she had a wild private life.

'I've been doing what most people do. I've been working.'

His brows shot towards his hairline. '*Working…you…?*'

'Yes, me, working. I was training to be a teacher when we met, if you remember.'

'Yes, but it was hardly your vocation; you gave it up without a second thought.'

Georgie's eyes widened as she scanned his face with incredulous anger. Didn't he realise that she'd have given up *anything* for him…that she'd have done *anything* he suggested without a second thought?

I must have been out of my mind!

'What choice did I have?'

Angolos looked exasperated. 'There is always a choice,' he rebutted.

She swallowed past the emotional congestion in her throat. 'You'd have been quite happy being married to a student, then?' she challenged.

'At no stage did you say your career was so important—'

'You're right, there is always a choice,' she interrupted. 'And I made the wrong one…I married you.'

The skin across his cheekbones tautened; his eyes meshed with hers. 'We both made the wrong choice.'

'Don't dwell on it; I didn't.' If you discounted the endless nights she had cried herself to sleep. 'I went back to college after Nicky was born.'

'A baby needs his mother.'

'That's what I always liked about you; you were so supportive of me.'

Angolos's astonished expression gave her a moment's amusement and for a second she felt like the empowered woman she wanted him to think her.

'For the record, Nicky has his mother; it's his father he

doesn't have,' she retorted, and had the pleasure of seeing a tell-tale wash of colour darken his golden-toned skin.

It would seem that at some level Angolos was aware that he had behaved like a despicable rat.

'*I* didn't reject him,' she continued. '*I'm* not the one who couldn't accept my responsibility.'

Angolos's nostrils flared as his glittering jet eyes locked onto those of his estranged wife.

'I didn't reject my son,' he rebutted thickly.

Georgie arched an ironic brow, outwardly at least oblivious to the waves of strong emotion he was projecting. She might once have turned herself inside out to pander to his moods, but that time was long gone.

'You and I must have very different interpretations of rejection.'

Angolos closed his eyes. The curse that escaped his clamped lips drew Georgie's attention to the sensual curve of his mouth. Her stomach dipped and she tore her eyes away.

'Sorry, but I don't understand Greek. Do you mind translating?'

'You don't understand my language because you made not the slightest effort to learn it.'

'No effort!' she yelped, stung by this unjust accusation. 'I may not have been very good, but it wasn't for want of trying. I only stopped going to the wretched lessons when—'

He looked at her in open amazement. 'Lessons? You did not take lessons.'

'Well, I had to do something to fill my days other than shopping and having my hair done.'

She had no intention of telling him that she had wanted to surprise him. That she had cherished an unrealistic ambition of casually replying to him in fluent, flawless Greek. Her ambition to make her husband proud of her seemed painfully pathetic in light of what had happened.

'So you were not content with your life as my wife?'

'You didn't want a wife, you wanted a mistress! And I'm not mistress material.' She watched an expression of astonishment steal across his face and added as a reckless afterthought, 'I was bored silly.'

CHAPTER SIX

'BORED…?'

Georgie turned a deaf ear to the dangerous note in Angolos's voice and nodded. 'Yes, bored. I got bored with you and Greek lessons.'

There was no way in the world she would ever tell him how his mother and sister had made fun of her attempts to converse. Angolos, they had said, would be embarrassed by her awkward grammar and appalling accent. Like all her attempts to fit in, this one had never stood a chance, not with in-laws who had never lost an opportunity to make her feel inadequate.

'I had no idea that living with me was such an ordeal.'

'Neither did I at the time. Now,' she told him calmly, 'I can be more objective.'

His eyes narrowed. 'So now your life is exciting and fulfilling?'

'I have a career and a child.'

'How did you take care of a baby and attend college?'

'I left him in the college crèche. And fortunately the school I work at is happy for him to go to the nursery there.'

'So you qualified…?'

'Amazing, isn't it? I'm actually not the brainless bimbo you and your family thought me, Angolos.'

His dark lashes swept downwards, touching the curve of his high, chiselled cheekbones as he studied his feet. There was a lengthy pause before he lifted his head and replied.

'I never thought you were brainless.'

Georgie did not make the mistake of taking this comment

as a compliment. She recognised that she was within seconds of losing control totally. Her assertions, the ones that she repeated like a mantra to herself every night, that she was totally over him, would be out the window if she started to batter her fists against his chest.

Their eyes locked and neither combatant heard the first tentative tap on the open door. The second, slighter louder one got their attention.

'I'll be right there, Ruth,' Georgie promised, pulling the door open.

'No hurry,' the older woman soothed. 'I'm sorry to disturb you, but Nicky is asking for his *cosy*. I wasn't sure what he meant.'

'It's his blanket, yellow…sort of. It's in his bedroom on the chest by the window.'

'He needs a security blanket?'

The faintest hint of criticism and her hackles were up. 'Actually it's a sheet.' So now he was the child expert.

'He has problems…?' A child who had been rejected by his father—why was he surprised? Angolos, a firm believer that a stable family was the only place to bring up a child, knew that if his son had problems the blame lay at his own door. He didn't know how this had happened, but he was a father and he needed to put right the harm he had already done.

'No, he doesn't have problems. He's a normal little boy who…' She stopped and frowned. 'Good grief, I don't know why I'm explaining anything to you of all people.'

'Because I am his father.'

'Biologically maybe…'

She had never expected her dig to evoke any real reaction, certainly not the expression of haunted regret that she saw on his face.

'Look, Angolos, if you've come over with a case of delayed

paternal feelings, I suggest you go take an aspirin or buy a shiny new car. I'm sure it will pass.'

'You think I am that shallow?' he enquired in a savage growl.

'Think? I *know* you're that shallow,' she retorted. 'Shallow and cruel and vindictive…' Something she might remind herself the next time she found herself in danger of feeling sorry for him. The fact was, if she ever started thinking of Angolos as the victim it was time for the men in white coats. 'This is a pointless conversation.'

'It's one we're going to have.'

Fine! If he wanted a war of attrition, she thought, he could have a war of attrition. But he was going to discover that during the time they'd been apart she had developed a backbone, not to mention a mind of her own!

'Why, Angolos? Because you say so? I know it used to work that way, but not any more.' She gave a hiss of frustration as her trained maternal ear caught the sound of her son's cry. A few seconds later Angolos heard it too and turned his head in the direction of the angry sound.

'What's wrong with him?'

'Being a mother doesn't make me psychic.' It had, however, given her the ability to distinguish between her son's cries. The one she had heard suggested tiredness, not pain or distress. 'I've got to go to him.' She started for the door, but he moved and effectively blocked her path with his body. Her nostrils flared as she caught the faint scent of the fragrance he used. Low in her belly her muscles tightened.

'*Fine!*' she snapped, throwing up her hands in angry capitulation. 'If you want me to listen to you I will, but not now or here.'

'When and where, then?'

She said the first thing that came into her head. 'The beach.'

'Where we used to meet. Where you offered me your innocence…'

His tone, softly sensual, stole the strength from her legs at the first syllable. Falling flat on her face would not be a good move, Georgie decided, reaching casually for the back of a conveniently placed chair. 'The way I recall it, you were pretty eager to take it.' Unfair, but she didn't feel inclined to fairness at that moment. 'I'll meet you tomorrow night at eight…'

Her family would be back then and Nicky would be safely tucked up in bed.

'And this time I won't be offering you anything.'

'Tonight.'

'I can't,' she began, and then saw his expression. 'All right, tonight,' she agreed with a sigh.

For a moment his narrowed eyes held hers, then he inclined his head. 'It would seem we have a date.'

'Hell,' she loudly announced to his back, 'will freeze over first.' She closed the front door and leaned against it with a sigh; she was shaking. With her luck, she thought, Angolos would construe her childish retort as a challenge—that would be just like him.

And what on earth was Angolos up to? she wondered as she sank weakly to the floor. She sat there, her back wedged against the door, her knees tucked under her chin, waiting for her knees to stop shaking. For once Nicky's need for attention came secondary; secondary to the necessity for her to be able to walk without falling over.

When she got to her feet she felt strangely numb, as though her stressed body had produced some natural anaesthetic. She didn't want to think about how she would feel when it wore off.

Georgie went through the rest of the day on autopilot. She tried hard to conceal the anxiety that lodged like a weight behind her breastbone but as the day progressed it got increasingly difficult.

Ruth, bless her, agreed to come over later and sit with Nicky. She didn't ask any questions and, beyond a searching look and a brief, 'Are you all right?' she had not asked anything about Angolos.

Georgie was grateful for her reticence. She knew if Gran had been there she would not have escaped so lightly. Her grandmother had barely managed to be civil to Angolos before they had split up. Who knew how she'd have reacted if she'd been here when he'd turned up?

Why, after years of conspicuous silence, was Angolos here? The question gnawed at her all day. It was when Nicky's lower lip trembled after she had snapped at him over something trivial that she decided enough was enough.

By letting Angolos get to her this way she was allowing him to win. After all, it didn't matter what he had to say, or why he was here, he wasn't part of her life any more. Ironically it was when she stopped looking for answers that she accidentally found one.

She discovered the innocent-looking envelope when she was performing the daily ritual of picking up Nicky's toys from the living room after he had gone to bed. She glanced incuriously at her name, and, assuming it was junk mail, aimed it at the waste-paper basket. It was only when it missed and she went to retrieve it from where it fell that she realised the paper was good quality.

She turned the envelope over. There was no stamp or postmark and it wasn't sealed. She opened it and slid out the contents. She immediately recognised the letterhead of the law firm that Angolos used. Crazy, really, that she should feel shocked—even crazier that she had to blink back the tears. This was something she had been expecting for the past three years. It was the logical step and one that her family had frequently urged her to take.

Angolos wanted a divorce.

*　　*　　*

'You look very nice, dear,' Ruth commented as she walked with Georgie to the front door.

'I'm wearing make-up,' Georgie admitted, lifting a self-conscious hand to her lightly glossed lips.

'Charming, but I was thinking of the dress.'

Georgie flushed, and looked down at the pale peach-coloured halter-necked dress she had finally selected. Even with her limited wardrobe it had taken her half an hour.

'It's too much, isn't it?' she fretted, smoothing the light fabric over her slender hips. 'I knew it was. I'll go and change.'

Ruth laughed. 'Don't be silly, you look lovely. Whether it's too much rather depends on what reaction you want to get?'

'I was aiming towards a sharp intake of breath,' Georgie admitted.

'Oh, I think you'll get that. I hope you don't mind me asking, but is there a reconciliation on the cards?'

'I don't mind you asking and, no, there isn't.'

If anyone had asked her yesterday if she nursed any hope of them ever getting back together, Georgie would have been able to give a very definite no way in reply, and mean it.

Yesterday she hadn't opened that envelope.

Reading the contents of a letter that explained with surgical precision that your husband wanted a divorce was a bad time to realise that in some secret corner of your heart you had clung onto hope. Foolish, irrational hope that one day... She took a deep breath. She knew that she was better off without that sort of hope.

'Actually, Angolos wants a divorce.' She had the horrid suspicion that her extremely casual attitude wasn't fooling Ruth for a minute. 'That's why he's come in person. I suspect there's someone else.' Maybe Sonia...? It would certainly please his family if he got back with his first wife.

If not Sonia, there would be someone. A highly sexed and

incredibly good-looking man like Angolos was never going to be celibate. She had come to terms with this.

Sure you have.

'I think it might be serious,' she heard herself say.

Ruth's brow furrowed. 'Now that *does* surprise me.'

'Not me; I've been expecting it.' Georgie gave her best carefree smile and wished she'd not revealed her suspicions to the older woman. 'The only thing that surprises me is it's taken him this long. Actually I think it'll be a good thing…making it official will give us proper closure.'

The other woman nodded and murmured agreement, but Georgie could see that she didn't believe a word. Embarrassed, she turned away. 'I won't be long,' she promised huskily.

About as long as it took to say goodbye.

CHAPTER SEVEN

ANGOLOS watched Georgie walk towards him along the beach with the graceful, long-legged stride he remembered so well. She carried her sandals in one hand slung over her shoulder in exactly the same way she always had. He was not a man inclined to nostalgia, but it was hard not to make a depressing comparison to the past.

Then, when she had caught sight of him her face would light up like a kid on Christmas morning and she would break into a run as though every second apart from him was one too many. Now when she saw him, and he recognised the precise moment, the only place she looked like running was in the opposite direction! You could almost hear her inner struggle as she covered the remaining distance.

Some irrational part of him wanted to make her smile at him that way again. Was it the same irrational part of him that had been tempted, albeit briefly, not to question her pregnancy? Then sense had prevailed and his pride had reasserted itself.

That he had contemplated, even for a moment, living a lie and bringing up another man's child, accepting his wife's infidelity, filled him with a profound self-disgust. Ironically of course it hadn't been another man's child she carried, but at the time he hadn't known that.

'Am I late?' Composed and utterly controlled, she sketched a smile. Her wary eyes, their incredible colour intensified by the soft shading on her eyelids, met his.

'No. I am early.'

Angolos didn't have a clue why her manner annoyed him

so much. It wasn't as if he had expected her to throw her arms around his neck and press her slim young body to his.

His eyes drifted towards the slim young body in question and he grew still. The summer dress exposed the soft, creamy contours of her satin-smooth shoulders and slim arms. The locket dangling from a slim gold chain suspended around her neck drew the attention to the firm swell of her breasts. As his glance moved lower the breeze caught the light fabric, drawing it close over her slim thighs.

Georgie had been so gut-churningly nervous that until his dark eyes swept over her she had forgotten that she had dressed to kill, or at least immobilise with lust—until his heavy-lidded, penetrating eyes lifted and met hers.

She had got the reaction she wanted, only this wasn't theoretical lust. A classic case, she remonstrated herself, of not considering the consequences. The smoky heat and raw hunger in his eyes—for a man who could be infuriatingly enigmatic, Angolos had eyes that could be quite devastatingly expressive on occasion—sent a current of sizzling heat through her body.

Experience had taught her how to fan the flames of his desire. She tried not to access the memories that reminded her of how pleasurable the results of her provocation could be. She raised a fluttering hand to her throat and tried to get her breathing under control.

'Can we get on? I'm on my way somewhere.' She was quite pleased with her clever subterfuge; now he wasn't going to think she had got dressed up for him.

She saw his jaw clench. 'I'm so glad you could fit me into your busy schedule.'

'Well, you didn't actually give me any choice, did you?' she reminded him.

'I don't suppose I did.' One dark brow arched. 'Aren't you a little cold dressed like that? Would you like my jacket?'

Her eyes widened in alarm. The thought of having the garment still carrying the warmth of his body, retaining the unique scent of him, next to her skin sent an illicit thrill through her body.

'No, I'm fine,' she promised hastily.

'As you wish. Would you like to go somewhere…for a coffee…a drink? Is that odd little teashop still open?'

The question brought back a flood of memories.

Odd, he had said. Well, as venues for conducting a passionate affair went, the quaint, touristy tearooms run by two elderly sisters had to be one of the most unlikely. They had frequently had the place to themselves. Most people had been outside enjoying the sun that summer, which had been just as well because inconspicuous they had not been—or at least he hadn't!

Not that Georgie had much cared about discretion; as far as she'd been concerned the entire town could talk. She had been too besotted to care about such things, and actually much to her frustration they hadn't actually had much to be discreet about!

After that first occasion when they had come as near as damn it to making love in the wet sand—*and I didn't even know his name*—Angolos had kept her at arm's length. Even though she hadn't been experienced she had sensed he'd been keeping himself under tight control. Georgie, who had fantasised about recreating the wild, primitive night-time encounter—minus the frustration—had bitterly regretted telling him that he was her first lover.

Instead of the passionate love-making Georgie had craved, for two weeks they had drunk tea and talked, or at least that was the way it had felt to her. They had taken long drives and talked. They had taken long walks and talked. It had been sheer agony, but she'd been prepared to endure any torture devised by man to be in his company.

The weekend two weeks later, when he'd disappeared without a word, she had thought that was it, and she had been totally devastated. The idea of never seeing him again had made the future stretch ahead of her bleak and barren.

She had drifted around like a ghost, grey-faced and drawn, but instead of recognising a broken heart her family had been irritated by her lethargy.

Then her grandmother had diagnosed anorexia—*She has all the classic symptoms*... The article she had read had apparently said that sufferers always lied, so Georgie's denials had been ignored.

Consequently, when Angolos had turned up out of the blue at the house two weeks later, instead of looking interestingly pale she had gained seven pounds!

He had formally requested her father's permission to marry her. Superficially it might have seemed a delightfully old-fashioned courtesy, but only *very* superficially.

Oh, he had been polite enough, but he had left no doubt that he had been going to marry her with or without her father's permission. *With* would simply be less problematic.

She was bowled over by his masterful behaviour; it hadn't even crossed Georgie's mind to question the fact he hadn't even asked her. My compliance he took for granted and why wouldn't he...?

She pushed aside the cringe-worthy recollection of her uncritical adoration; she had held nothing back. She hadn't just worn her heart on her sleeve, she had stripped her soul bare!

'No, I don't want tea, I just want this over with as quickly as possible.' She kept her voice cool and unemotional and was rewarded by the surprise flicker in the back of his deep-set eyes.

'You can't spare a few minutes to discuss our son's future...?'

'I would spare a lot more than a few minutes to discuss Nicky's future, but not with you,' she retorted, bristling with antagonism. 'Nicky is nothing to do with you, and don't pretend you're really interested in him,' she sneered.

His expression tautened. 'Be reasonable.'

'Reasonable!' she yelled back, no longer able to contain the anger and resentment that she'd been storing up for these long years. 'Reasonable the way you were when you said you didn't want to know about the baby?' she demanded in a low, impassioned voice. 'Are you on medication, Angolos?'

'Do not raise your voice to me.' His own voice was low and angry.

'If the worst I do is raise my voice you'll leave here a fortunate man.'

He absorbed her angry words in thoughtful silence. 'You have developed quite a temper,' he observed, his glance drifting from her flushed, furious face to her fists clenched tightly at her sides.

'I *always* had a temper.' It was odd, she mused, that a man who knew her more intimately than any other man, a man who was the father of her child, should actually not know her very well at all.

His harsh scowl melted to something far more dangerous as their eyes meshed. 'Maybe you should have revealed this aspect of your character when we were together. It suits you.'

'I should have done a lot of things when we were together, including walking out before you so charmingly threw me out!'

The colour that began low on his throat travelled upwards until his entire face was suffused. 'I could have done that better,' he admitted huskily.

'Is that your version of grovelling?' She gave her head an impatient shake. 'Even if you crawled on your hands and knees I'd never forgive you for what you did.'

His face had that closed, unreadable expression as he said tautly, 'I think I should tell you why I asked you to—'

He's going to say it. *Divorce*…once he said it, it would be real. She suddenly went icy cold. Maybe I'm not ready to hear this after all…?

How long do you need…?

'I know why you're here,' she cut in quickly.

His dark brows drew together in a straight line above his masterful nose. *'You do…?'*

'For goodness' sake, don't drag it out. I need to get back.' She raised her wrist and evinced astonishment at the hour, even though she couldn't see her watch through the warm mist of unshed tears.

'You kept it.'

Her shimmering gaze lifted. 'Kept what?'

Angolos tapped the diamond-encrusted face of the watch he had bought her on their honeymoon. His hand dropped away, but not before the tips of his long brown fingers had trailed lightly along the inner aspect of her slender wrist.

It was barely a touch yet her body reacted like that of an addict given the scent of her drug of choice, only to have it snatched away. Inside the loose cotton bodice her breasts ached and craved the touch of hands and lips. Buried memories resurfaced and the ache low in her pelvis became a physical pain.

'I'm sentimental that way.' Let him never know how true that was.

The week in Paris, their honeymoon, had been utter bliss; she treasured the memory of every single moment of it. She had been a nervous bride the first night, but the moment he had touched her she had quickly lost her inhibitions. Her introduction into a sensual world she hadn't known existed had left her in a daze. Every morning when she'd woken up tangled up with the warm, lithe body of her incredible lover she'd felt as if she had died and gone to heaven.

For a week everything had been magical. Georgie had tried, but had never been able to recapture that magic.

The first cracks had appeared when they'd arrived in Greece. It had been here that the scale of Angolos's wealth had hit Georgie for the first time. They had landed on his private heli-pad, for goodness' sake! In her world people who had two cars were well off; Angolos had casually revealed that he had a yacht, which was presently being refitted.

From the air she had been able to see that the estate, located on a peninsula, covered acres and acres. The main house itself and the gorgeously landscaped grounds with their tennis courts and pools were palatial, and the setting beside the sea was totally stunning.

'Not disappointed, are you?' Angolos had teased.

'It's all incredible.' *So was a museum.*

Georgie, who had been brought up in a standard 1930s semi-detached house, was actually daunted by the sheer scale of everything. She had thought there might be a housekeeper or some help in the garden, but to discover there was an army of live-in domestic help to run the place came as a nasty shock.

This wasn't the sort of house where you nipped down to the kitchen to make yourself a sandwich in the middle of the night. She seriously doubted that Angolos knew where the kitchens were!

Within ten seconds she knew that she wasn't going to acclimatise to her new life overnight. It was going to be a steep learning curve, but she reasoned if she had Angolos there to help her she would be all right. She didn't know at the time that he wouldn't be…that his work would occupy most of his waking moments.

She walked around the place making the right admiring noises, but she couldn't imagine ever thinking of this place as home. And on top of that there was his family, who had been there in force when she'd arrived.

'Sorry about tonight,' Angolos said when they lay in bed later that night. 'They wanted to inspect my new bride, and who,' he suggested throatily, 'can blame them?'

'I don't think they were very impressed.'

'Don't be silly. They'll love you…why wouldn't they?'

Angolos impatiently dismissed her concerns. 'You just need to relax a little.'

'You don't think I was relaxed… Did I come over as—?'

He laid a finger against her lips. 'Forget about my family; it doesn't matter what they think. They'll be gone tomorrow.'

She breathed a sigh of relief. Angolos seemed different in this environment, but she was sure that once they were alone everything would be all right. She couldn't wait.

'Good…that is, I'm sure they're very nice, but there was an awful lot of them.' There was no way she was going to remember the names of all those aunts and uncles and cousins. As Angolos was kissing his way up her neck she was hard-pressed to remember her own name.

'I really don't want to talk about relatives,' he said, pausing halfway up.

'Me neither,' she admitted huskily as he peeled off her transparent nightgown to reveal glowing skin.

'*Theos*, but you are beautiful.'

His words drove everything else from Georgie's mind. She melted.

The sex was spectacular, but the problem was still there the next day in the shape of his mother and sister. They were still there at lunch-time.

Short of packing their bags for them, what could she do?

As she walked out to the helicopter pad with Angolos, who had explained he had to go into the office, she took the opportunity to casually enquire, 'When are your mother and sister going home?'

Angolos threw some instruction to his assistant, a polite, nice-looking young man who was distantly related. As the younger man hurried ahead Angolos directed a puzzled frown at Georgie's face.

'*Home…?*' He shook his head. 'I don't follow.'

'I was wondering when your mother and Sacha were going back home.'

He threw back his head and laughed. 'They are home, *yineka mou*, didn't I say? They live here.'

Somehow the strained smile stayed glued to her face. 'No, you didn't say.' The realisation that they would be sharing a home with his family made her spirits plummet. It had taken about five minutes for her to realise that she and her mother-in-law were never going to be pals, and that her sister-in-law, whom Georgie considered horribly indulged, looked down her aristocratic little nose at her.

'Mother will be a big help while you're settling in, and Sacha is your age—you're bound to have a lot in common.'

Georgie, who seriously doubted either of these claims, responded to the kiss he planted on her lips with less enthusiasm than previously.

'Are you all right?'

Georgie, a big fan of telling it as it was, heard herself lie. 'Terrific…just a bit tired.'

That was the first time she concealed her feelings from him, but not the last time. She even got quite good at it though her acting talents were stretched to the limit when he dropped one particular bombshell on her.

Angolos went to Paris, this time on business and without her. 'I'd love for you to come with me, of course I would, but this is business. You do understand…?'

On his return he casually mentioned, in a 'you'll never guess who I bumped into' sort of way, that he had had dinner with his ex-wife while there.

Georgie, who had already been force-fed a daily dose of Sonia-worship by her in-laws, wanted to scream, but instead she smiled and said quietly, 'How nice.'

The following month he announced he had invited Sonia up for the weekend. That his ex arrived late seemed to be taken for granted. Georgie could have accommodated her tardiness, but she could never forgive their guest for being poised, self-assured and, it went without saying, drop-dead gorgeous. In fact she had all the qualities necessary to be Angolos's wife—heck, she even still had her ring; she'd just swapped fingers!

In other words she was everything Georgie longed to be and wasn't.

She was also very tactile, always touching and stroking. Georgie was forced to watch as she stroked Angolos's arm or ran her fingers over his lean cheek. It seemed to Georgie that every time she walked into a room they were there, laughing in a corner, sharing their jokes and their secrets. Feeling totally alienated, she retreated into her shell.

'You never struck me as sentimental.'

She turned her head towards Angolos and smiled. Unexpectedly recalling the traumatic events made her realise just how much she had changed in the intervening years. It was quite an empowering experience to realise that if she found herself in that situation today she would not creep away to feel slighted and sorry for herself in the corner.

No, she would tell the other woman to lay off. She would confront Angolos—at best his behaviour was insensitive, at worst he still had feelings for his ex. She would demand he decided whom he wanted, because she wasn't playing second fiddle to anyone!

'I was being ironic. The watch—' she glanced at her wrist '—is a good investment, much more likely to rise in value than money in the bank, or so I was told.' By her dad when he'd returned the watch, having taken it to be valued without her knowledge.

'You had it valued?'

She nodded; her father had been shocked that she'd been walking around wearing something that was, as he'd put it, 'worth as much as a two-bedroomed house', without any insurance.

'My finances were tight.'

'You seem to have a more practical attitude to money than you once did.'

'Practical?' She thought about the wild flowers, carefully pressed and preserved alongside other treasures in the velvet-lined box. Angolos had picked them for her the first time they'd walked through the sand dunes. 'I'm working on it. But I don't think I'll ever care about money for its own sake and I don't put a price on things the way you do.'

'Not even your virginity?'

Heat flooded her face as her furious flashing eyes flew to his face. 'Don't you dare make out I held out to make you marry me!' she snapped. 'You always put a higher value on that than I did,' she reminded him. 'You could have had it for nothing, Angolos—you didn't have to marry me.'

In the long simmering silence their eyes locked. His chest lifted as he expelled a long sibilant sigh.

'I know.' She would never know what it had cost him not to accept what she had been so anxious to give him.

'Then why…?'

He pressed his fingers to the groove above his masterful nose and scanned the stretch of beach. It was empty but for a few people walking dogs.

'Why did you marry me, Angolos?'

'Do you want to walk?'

She released a hiss of frustration through clenched teeth. 'You've no intention of telling me, have you?'

The disturbing smile that played around the corners of his sensual lips neither confirmed nor denied her husky accusation. *'Walk…?'*

'Walk?' In contrast to the restive energy that Angolos was projecting, she felt utterly drained.

'You know—put one foot in front of the other.'

It really ought to be that simple, but her shaking knees didn't have the strength or co-ordination to move her from the spot. 'You're impossible,' she accused.

'But cute?' he suggested.

She only just stopped herself responding to his smile. 'I never thought I'd hear you say "cute".'

'Is that a yes?'

'No.'

One winged dark brow arched. 'No to cute or a walk?'

'Both.' She sat down rather hurriedly.

'As you wish.'

Angolos followed suit but with less haste and considerably more grace. As she tucked her knees under herself and arranged her skirt around her legs Georgie was aware of his dark eyes watching her. She was aware of just about everything about him, including the warm male scent that made her oversensitive nostrils twitch.

'Don't try and charm me, Angolos. I've got immunity. Anyway, you've no need to butter me up. Like I said, I already know what this is about.'

Her head lifted, their eyes connected. Angolos's expression was wary; it cost her a supreme effort to smile. 'Don't worry, I'm not going to make a fuss, if that's what you're worried about.'

Angolos looked at the envelope she handed him but made no effort to take it.

'I think I've signed all the places I need to.'

He still didn't react, just carried on looking at it with a total lack of recognition in his eyes.

'For heaven's sake.' She leant across and deposited it in his lap. 'I found it, it must have fallen out of your pocket. Did you think you'd lost it?'

He took the envelope and turned it over in his hand cautiously as though he expected it to burst into flames. Georgie found his manner bewildering.

'*Dios*, I had totally forgotten about this.' After his meeting with Paul he had contacted his lawyer. The papers were already prepared; they had been for two years.

'How long will it take to be…final? The d…divorce.'

CHAPTER EIGHT

ANGOLOS'S glance lifted to Georgie's face. There was a strange look in his deep-set eyes that she couldn't interpret. *'Never!'*

The forcefulness of his explosive retort made her stare at him in confusion. 'I don't understand.'

'Then understand this.' Georgie gave a grunt of shock as he began to tear the envelope into pieces with slow, deliberate thoroughness before tossing them up into the air.

She watched in open-mouthed astonishment as the fragments went flying down the beach in several directions, drifting like confetti on the air currents.

'Have you gone mad?' She turned her astounded eyes on him. 'Why make the effort to bring that here personally and then do that?'

'I never intended…'

'Never intended what?' she prompted.

His jaw tightened. 'We're not getting divorced.'

She pressed her hands to her head, the dull throb in her temples had turned into a blinding headache. 'But you came here to…and I *want* to get divorced!' she added on a note of escalating misery.

'Too bad.'

'*You* want to get divorced.' The squally sea breeze suddenly caught her skirt and lifted it. It took her several moments to smooth it back down, and when she looked up she saw something in his eyes that made her sensitive stomach flip.

'You saw Paul at his surgery.'

Georgie didn't want to talk about Paul. 'So that's how you knew we were here.'

Angolos inclined his dark head.

'I know some people think strong and silent is attractive, but ask them how they feel about it after they've lived with strong and silent for a few weeks. I think you'd find they'd have changed their tune,' she predicted grimly. 'For goodness' sake, don't just look all brooding and beautiful—*say something*!'

His only response to her emotional outburst was a raised eyebrow—one of these days she would swing for this man.

'What would you like me to say?'

'I give up!' she declared. She slid an exasperated sideways glance at his lean, saturnine profile. 'What were you doing discussing me with Paul anyway?' she demanded crossly. 'He has no right to discuss me; there's such a thing as patient confidentiality.'

Angolos dismissed her complaint with an impatient motion of his hand. 'I'm your husband.'

'On paper.' Paper that was even now blowing across the ocean…her divorce would probably end up in Normandy. 'And even if we were together, that doesn't give you a right to know my medical details.'

'He didn't divulge any private details, medical or otherwise,' Angolos cut in impatiently. 'He told me I have a son.'

She dug her toe into the sand and vented an ironic laugh. 'That was news…?'

'To me it was.'

'How can you say that?'

He ignored her exasperated exclamation. 'Now I know that Nicky is mine, obviously things must change.'

Her eyes narrowed. 'Two words I'm not liking there… "must" and "change".'

'Don't be obtuse, Georgette. You know where I'm going with this.'

She shook her head. 'Not a clue.'

'Then I'll spell it out: we will be a family.'

The bad feeling in her stomach coalesced into straightforward panic. 'I have all the family I need.' He wasn't…he just *couldn't* be suggesting what she thought he was!

'A family requires both parents. You and Nicky will come back to Greece with me and we will be a family.'

A hoarse laugh was drawn from Georgie's aching throat. 'And to think I used to be intimidated by your vast intellect. You know, mostly I was scared stiff of giving an opinion in case you laughed at me.'

Angolos looked so appalled by this confidence that under less fraught circumstances she might have laughed.

'But now I know that you may be clever, but you're also stark staring crazy. *Me live with you again…?* The only way you'll get me back to Greece is in a strait-jacket.'

'You're speaking emotionally without considering—'

'I don't need to consider anything. I recognise insanity when I hear it.'

Until he captured her wrists in his she wasn't aware that she had been tugging at her own hair. 'Calm down. You're overreacting.'

He acknowledged her snarling, *'shut up!'* with an infuriatingly tolerant smile.

'Once you've thought about it—' he continued talking across her demand to be *let go!* '—I think you'll come to appreciate that this is the right thing to do. Sometimes being a parent involves sacrifice.'

He really was incredible. '*You're* telling *me* that? Know a lot about being a parent, do you? Gosh, share your wisdom, I'm all ears,' she begged.

Her sarcasm drew a soft expletive from his lips. 'You are—' A dark line appeared across the slashing curve of his cheekbones as he swallowed the rest of his furious retort. 'You can mock as much as you like.' The fingers encircling her wrists tightened and then, much to her intense relief, fell away completely.

'Thanks, but I don't need your permission.'

'But,' he continued as though she hadn't spoken, 'it doesn't alter the fact that a child needs both parents.'

'I can tell you from personal experience that you can get by perfectly well with one.'

'You have your stepmother.'

Her brows lifted. 'And who's to say that at some future date Nicky won't have a stepfather…?'

There was a short, stark silence, during which the muscles in Angolos's brown throat rippled convulsively. Then, capturing her defiant eyes, he smiled and lifted his dark head to an imperious angle. 'I am to say,' he responded simply.

The scornful retort died on her lips as she encountered the chilling determination in his unblinking eyes.

'So now you're going to vet my boyfriends, are you? I'd be interested in how that works.'

'This isn't about you. This is about what is best for our son.'

More absurd than him trying to make her feel guilty and selfish was the fact she actually did! 'I've been doing the best for our son for the past three years. What have you been doing for him? On second thoughts, you staying out of his life probably was the biggest favour you could do him.'

He visibly paled in response to her vitriolic attack, but didn't attempt to defend himself. 'I can understand your anger.'

'I doubt that, I really doubt that,' she gritted. 'And besides, I don't want your understanding.' What did she want from him? Was she going to be happier if he walked away? She fixed him with a resentful glare. 'I wish you'd never come.'

'Has it occurred to you that you are denying him his heritage?'

This change of tack increased her growing sense of unease.

'You're the one who denied him that. Besides, Nicky is perfectly happy where he is.'

'He doesn't even speak his own language.'

'His language is English.' She winced to hear both the defensiveness and doubt in her voice.

'Nicky is half Greek. He will only have to look in the mirror to see that.'

'I'm not trying to hide his heritage from him.'

'Aren't you?'

'No, I'm not. I would never lie to my son.'

'*Our* son.'

Gritting her teeth, Georgie refused to respond to the correction.

'He will know when he goes to school that he does not look like the fair-skinned children in his class. What will you say when he asks you why he is different?'

'You obviously know very little about the ethnic mix in most schools, if you think that Nicky will stand out. Have you never heard of a multicultural society?'

One dark brow angled. 'So what will you do when he asks about me?'

'I…I haven't thought about it.'

'Don't you think it's about time you did?'

She lifted her resentful eyes to his. 'Nicky's happy,' she contended stubbornly.

Angolos studied her face. 'You know I'm right, don't you, Georgette?' Before she had a chance to deny his assertion he added, 'And I can see that Nicky is happy.'

Her hopes rose, only to be dashed.

'However, I will not permit my son to be brought up not knowing who his father is…thinking that he is unwanted…' He swallowed hard, the muscles of his throat contracting as he visibly struggled to control his feelings. 'The boy is being brought up surrounded by women…'

'And what's wrong with women?'

His face relaxed briefly into a slow smile. 'I like women…'

'Tell me something I don't know.' And they liked him. Everywhere they had gone together women's eyes had followed him—that he had seemed for the most part oblivious to the fact had been no comfort to her at the time.

'But a boy needs a male role model?'

Feeling increasingly on the defensive because of his uncomfortable ability to come up with a reply for everything she said, Georgie set her chin on her steepled fingers. 'There are plenty of men in Nicky's life.'

The fire in his dark eyes provided a stark contrast to the icy expression of austere disdain that spread across his lean face.

'I have no wish to be regaled with your romantic adventures. Nicky does not need *men* in the plural…'

The criticism struck her as the height of hypocrisy. 'I'm not the one who has trouble forming stable relationships… And who did you have in mind as a role model?' Her feathery brows lifted. 'You? Don't make me laugh,' she pleaded with contempt.

Angolos's expression was glacial as he responded. 'You have someone you consider more suitable in mind?'

Her chin lifted. 'And if I do?' she challenged pugnaciously.

'If you do, Georgette, I would advise you not to pursue that very dangerous course.'

Her chest swelled with outrage. 'Is that a threat?'

His silky smile sent a shiver down her rigid spine, but it was the fluttery sensation low in her stomach that sent her several steps closer to outright panic.

'Threats are for wimps.'

A hissing sound of disgust issued from her pursed lips. 'That is *exactly* the sort of macho posturing I don't want my son exposed to.'

'*Our* son.'

Their combative stares locked and the seconds ticked by. Georgie was the first to break the lengthening silence.

'You can't just walk back into my life this way, Angolos…' She turned away, her face scrunched up in anguish as the fight drained from her body. 'It's not fair.'

'Only children expect life to be fair.' The unexpected note of sympathy in his voice brought a lump to her aching throat.

'It rather depends on their experience.' Her lips curved upwards, but there was no smile in her eyes as she added, 'You forget that my mother walked out when I was a baby.'

'No, I remember.' He dragged a hand through his hair. 'Your grandmother will be pleased to see us reunited.'

'Don't talk like it's a done deal, Angolos,' she warned, managing a weak smile at his irony.

'But you agree that a stable family environment is the best place to bring up a child.'

'Of course I do; I'm not stupid.' Georgie forced her clenched fists to relax. 'I need time to think. This is just too much…too soon…'

'We were good together…you must remember…'

Her eyes flew wide open as anger surged through her body—other things surged too, but she concentrated hard on the anger.

'So *good*, in fact, that you threw me out.'

Unable to hold her accusing gaze, Angolos brought his dark lashes down in a concealing screen. 'I am not proud…'

'I don't much care about your precious pride or regret or anything else!' she declared hotly. 'The fact is you rejected our baby… So you want to be a family now—' her slender shoulders lifted '—big deal! Next year or next week even you'll probably have changed your mind again. Do you think I'd put my future and that of my son in the hands of someone so…who can't make up his mind what he wants?'

'I know exactly what I want.'

His low, throaty declaration sent a jolt of sharp sexual

awareness through her body. 'Yes, you want your own way,' she contended without looking at him. Looking at him would be a *very* bad idea just now.

'I want us to be a family and I think you do too.'

She angled a narrow-eyed look at his face. 'That was what I thought we were four years ago. Give me one reason why I should ever believe what you say to me? You've never even told me why! All I got was a shrug and a sneer and c…coldness.' She stopped and bit her lip to control the quiver in her voice.

'All I want to know is *why*…'

'Well, for starters, I knew that you were sleeping with someone else.'

A long throbbing silence developed.

'Not *that* again,' she said wearily. 'Not even *you* are that stupid. Sure…sure I had a string of lovers.'

The expression she saw cross his face suggested this wasn't the response he had been expecting. 'I had proof.'

'*That* I would really like to see.'

'You've got nerve, I'll give you that,' he gritted back. 'But you were not as careful as you thought.'

'Come on, Angolos, I'm not listening unless you tell me the real reason you rejected Nicky.'

His beautiful mouth twisted as their eyes touched. 'I was prepared…I actually thought we might be able to get beyond your infidelity,' he recalled. 'I blamed myself for leaving you alone.'

'You were going to forgive me!' This got even more implausible. 'If you seriously thought there was another man you would have torn him limb from limb,' she contended.

He gave an odd, twisted smile. 'You'd have thought so, wouldn't you?'

'So what's the *real* reason?'

Above the sound of the waves crashing softly on the sand

she heard his white teeth grating. 'Be honest,' she recommended.

'*Me*, honest?'

'A baby didn't fit in with your life then, did it?' she claimed, ignoring his raw interjection. 'I don't know what's changed, but now you've suddenly decided—'

He pressed his hand to his mouth and shook his dark head. '*Theos!*' he thundered, eyeing her with frustrated incredulity. His chest rose and fell in tune to his rapid, uneven respirations. 'I knew I couldn't have children.'

CHAPTER NINE

THE only sound to disturb the silence that followed Angolos's driven declaration was the cracking noise as he clenched his long fingers and the audible hiss of his laboured breathing.

'Not have children...?' Georgie shot a sideways look at his taut profile. 'You're not making any sense.'

'I was told that I couldn't have children.'

She just stared at him, hearing, but not able to digest what he had said.

'Do you understand what I'm saying?'

She pressed her fingers to her temples and shook her head. 'No.'

'Evidently I was wrong.'

'But it's silly—you couldn't...' Angolos was so rampantly male he couldn't be... She shook her head positively and without thinking her eyes dropped down his body. 'You're—'

'I am functional,' he cut in. 'You're confusing sterility with impotence.'

Flushing to the roots of her hair at his sardonic intervention, she jerked her eyes back to his face.

'I just didn't think I was capable of fathering a child.'

'But we'd only been together a few weeks. You couldn't know that unless—' *Unless he had already tried to have a baby.* With someone else. With Sonia. The colour suddenly leached dramatically from her lightly tanned skin. 'Oh,' she said swallowing. 'I see.'

So now she had the answer to the question that had puzzled many people at the time. Namely, why should a couple so supremely well suited as Sonia and Angolos get divorced?

This new revelation provided the answer, and Georgie could see how it could have happened. They had desperately wanted a family, and Sonia hadn't got pregnant.

It wouldn't be the first time the strain of that sort of situation had split up a marriage.

She could see it all: Sonia had thrown herself into a mad social whirl, and Angolos had buried himself in his work. They wouldn't have talked, of course…as she knew to her cost Angolos didn't talk.

You had only to witness Sonia and Angolos together to see that they still had feelings for one another. And Georgie had witnessed them together. She hadn't had much choice when the woman had been their house guest barely weeks after they had married.

'So when I said I was pregnant…some men might have thought it was a miracle, but you thought that I…'

Some men hadn't had a letter written by their wife's lover in their possession. Even after all these years the humiliation of that discovery was still with him. 'I suppose some men might, but that is all in the past, now I know…'

'And now you know you can have children.'

Right result, wrong mother.

Was that what he had thought when he realised…? Had he wondered why this couldn't have happened while he was with Sonia?

Georgie pressed the heel of one hand to the centre of her chest where misery had lodged like a solid object behind her breastbone. Would the pain ever go away…?

'Yes, now I know I have a child. I have Nicky, and I want to be his father.'

A furrow appeared in her smooth brow. 'No.' She wouldn't deprive Nicky of his father, but how could she survive with Angolos as part of her life? If she had ever kidded herself she weren't as madly in love with him as ever, she recognised now that this convenient self-delusion was no longer an option.

He slid her a burning look of impatience. 'What do you mean, no?'

'I mean…I don't know what I mean.' She shook her head. 'No, this can't be right. We talked about having a family…we planned…' She stopped and realised that they hadn't talked; *she* had talked. Her stomach lurched sickly as the implications of his confession hit her. 'You knew about this when we got married?'

'I did.'

'And you didn't tell me—you let me think…'

Angolos watched the colour drain from her face; the sprinkling of freckles across her nose stood out against the marble pallor. 'You *can't* love them,' she had always said when he had told her he loved those freckles.

'You let me talk about babies when all along…' A shudder ran through her body as she turned her tearful, accusing eyes to his face. 'Why didn't you tell me? You let me carry on thinking…'

'It was an omission, and I was wrong.' A man with an ounce of integrity would have given her the opportunity to make an informed decision.

In his own defence he had fully planned to tell her before the wedding. He had lost count of the number of times that he had started to tell her only to pull back at the last moment.

He had rationalised it, of course, told himself that she was marrying *him*… After all, her inability to give him a child wouldn't have altered his feelings.

Feelings were the core of the problem…

She had lit up when he'd walked into a room; she had shaken when he'd touched her. Angolos had known full well that she had been infatuated with him. Young and infatuated, but *love*…? Had he dared put it to the test?

'I'm sorry, Angolos.'

His startled eyes flew to her face.

Georgie was pale but composed. As he watched she pushed the hair back from her face with her forearm. It was an intensely weary gesture. The urge to reach out and take her in his arms was so strong that for a moment he couldn't drag air into his lungs.

'What are you sorry for, *yineka mou*?'

'Well, it must have been incredibly hard for someone like you to be told that you couldn't father children.'

'Someone like me…?'

She nodded and as she lifted her eyes to his she caught the strangest expression crossing his face. 'Well, any man, then,' she moderated, tactfully not touching on his overdeveloped male pride. 'When they told you…' Her voice faded as she imagined him sitting in a clinical white office having the shattering news broken to him by an unsympathetic doctor. 'You must have felt like someone had kicked you in…' Her glance dropped and dark, fiery colour rose up her neck until her face was glowing. 'Sorry, that wasn't—'

'You're right, that's exactly how I felt,' Angolos cut in, taking pity on her.

'And I don't expect you discussed it with anyone.'

His smile faded. 'It is not the sort of thing a man discusses.'

His stiff pronouncement was exactly what she had been talking about. 'Point proven. You're really into all this macho stuff in a big way. There's no good denying it,' she added. 'And I know you can't help it. I'm just sorry,' she admitted with sigh, 'that you didn't feel able to confide in me, but then that was always the problem, wasn't it?

'You never treated me like an adult capable of making my own decisions. You always kept me out of the loop. Ours was never an equal relationship,' she reflected, contemplating her neatly trimmed, unpolished nails with a wistful expression that unknown to her had a more dramatic impact on Angolos than the kick she had previously so accurately described.

His expression had grown increasingly shocked as he listened to her matter-of-fact analysis of their relationship. By the time she finished he had the stunned aspect of someone who had just been hit by a runaway truck.

'I never expected you to take it this way.'

'Well, I'm not saying I would have been happy about it. I desperately wanted to have your baby.' She looked up and surprised a stricken expression on his lean face that cut her to the core. 'But it wouldn't have changed anything, not essentially,' she added firmly.

'You think not?'

His scepticism annoyed her. 'Yes, I do. We could have adopted...' Her face brightened. 'There are a lot of babies out there who need a home,' she told him earnestly.

'It would seem,' he said slowly, 'that I underestimated you.'

'When were you going to tell me?'

'I honestly don't know,' he admitted.

Truth be told, he had been willing to ignore every precept of decency that had been instilled in him all his life in order to marry a woman he hadn't even believed loved him, and now it seemed that woman's feelings had been deeper and less selfish than his own.

And he had blown it big time.

'At the moment our feelings for each other are not important,' he began in a voice totally devoid of emotion.

She pulled herself onto her knees and brushed the sand from her skirt with slow, deliberate strokes. 'Neither are they any mystery,' she said dully. To her way of thinking, if he had ever felt a shred of true feeling for her, he would never have sent her away.

She experienced a sudden swell of emotion. After everything he had done she still loved him and would continue to love him to her dying breath. The injustice of it all hit her.

Why should he not know what he had done to her? Why should she spare him?

'Do you want to know how I feel about you?'

A muscle along Angolos's taut jaw clenched. 'We will discuss your feelings for me at a more appropriate moment, when you are less emotional.'

'Which, roughly translated, means when you say so—no change there, then.'

The muscle clenching in his lean cheek reminded her of a ticking time bomb. Georgie supposed she *ought* to be grateful that his response had spared her from making a total fool of herself. All the same she couldn't help but think that it would be an enormous relief to get it all out into the open.

'Our son's future is what we must decide.'

'Nothing to decide.' Externally at least she maintained the appearance of control.

Actually his comment had terrified her. If there was one thing she had learnt from her short time with the Constantine clan, it was not to underestimate the power of money! Angolos might never get custody of Nicky—access was another story—but he could tear her life to shreds while he was trying.

'I beg to differ.'

'You never beg,' she cut back bitterly. 'You had your chance to be a father, Angolos, and you blew it. And look at it this way—there's nothing to stop you going out there and making babies with someone else.'

Her comment brought a gleam of pure fury to his eyes. 'You think I'm going to leave it like this?'

Her slender shoulders lifted. 'Why not?'

'I don't want babies, I want…Nicky.'

She drew her knees up to her chest and rested her chin on them. 'You don't always get what you want, Angolos.'

'Wake up, Georgette,' he recommended harshly. 'This is the real world.'

'No, your world isn't my reality. My world doesn't have designer dresses and glitzy first nights, or people who judge you by how much money you have and who your parents are!' she declared hotly. 'My reality is making ends meet, a good day at work, a parking space in the high street, scraped knees, temper tantrums and doctor's appointments.' She stopped to catch her breath. The incoherent inventory of her life made it sound less attractive than it actually was.

'All I'm asking for is a chance to be part of that world.'

It would seem Angolos hadn't picked up on the unattractive part.

Taken aback by the intensity of his unexpected request, she stared at him warily. Perhaps I should have added sleepless nights and guilt. Guilt was a major part of parenting that all the literature skimmed over.

'This isn't a glamorous world we are talking here.'

'*Glamour!*' He dismissed it with a contemptuous click of his long fingers. 'If anyone was seduced by the so-called glamour of my world, it was you,' he contended.

Her eyes widened in protest. 'That's a stupid thing to say.'

'Wasn't the fact I came from a different world than you part of the attraction?' he challenged. 'You put me on a pedestal!' he accused. 'And I exploited it.'

'I didn't feel exploited.' She didn't like the idea his comment created that she'd been some sort of victim walking blindly to her fate.

'The moments from our time together that remain clearly in my mind are not the lavish parties or dinners.'

'What are they, then?' She was probably going to regret asking, but if she didn't the question would plague her for the rest of her life.

'That picnic we had sitting cross-legged on the bedroom floor…'

Georgie's eyes widened. It had been the one time when she had dared the wrath of the kitchen staff and made a personal request. When asked what sort of wine she'd wanted with her fish-paste sandwiches she had said any old thing would do…white and fizzy maybe…?

The horror etched on the face of the chef had been comical. Of course the sandwiches had been smoked salmon, the wine had been champagne, and the cutlery Georgian silver, but she hadn't quibbled. Instead she had pronounced herself delighted, and thanked the staff warmly.

'You remember that?' she asked, astonished.

'Of course I damn well remember. I also remember what followed it—more so…' He studied her unblinkingly through eyes that contained an explicitly sexual message.

It was a message that Georgie received. The pupils of her eyes dilated dramatically until they almost swallowed up the amber. Breathing fast and shallow, she traced the outline of her dry lips with the tip of her tongue and drew a long shuddering breath. Her hand came up in a fluttery gesture and then fell away again, leaving her fingers trailing in the sand.

'*Do you…?*'

'You know I do.' She screwed up her eyes and tried to ignore the slick heat between her thighs. 'We had some good times,' she admitted huskily.

'A bit better than *good*.'

He was right. Good was safe and comfortable; what they had enjoyed had been neither. 'Think about it, Angolos,' she appealed to him. The glint in his eyes suggested he wasn't in the mood for thinking. 'Nothing has changed, not essentially. You came here to get a divorce.'

This did get his attention.

'I came here to find out the truth,' he rebutted.

'And I bet you wish you hadn't found it.'

'Wishes do not enter into it,' he told her, his voice low and controlled. 'I have a son… *Dios mio*!' he gasped, no longer the least bit controlled. His blazing eyes locked with hers. 'My life has changed profoundly. If you imagine even for one second that I would prefer to live in ignorance you are insane. I have a son. I may be slow but I do recognise a miracle when I see one.'

'You can have more children. Like I said, go and have a baby with someone else,' she recommended, fixing him with a belligerent glare. 'That's what you really want,' she contended. 'Nicky already has a family.'

She knew enough Greek to recognise that the low, impassioned flood that issued from his lips would have been severely censored by even the most liberal of censors. 'You think a solution would be for me to go away and impregnate another woman?'

'Frankly I'm amazed you haven't already. Or,' she added with a sneer, 'have you been waiting to be officially single?'

His nostrils flared as he scanned her face with distaste. 'Yes.'

In the act of brushing a wayward strand of hair from her face, Georgie froze. All expression was wiped from her face. 'I take it that is some kind of joke.'

'Actually, no, it isn't. I take the matrimonial vows quite seriously.'

'Oh, really? Your vows mentioned a bit of cherishing, and I seem to recall when you chucked me out there wasn't much cherishing involved. Don't feel bad about it,' she said. 'Some good came out of it. I have to admit, after not having a say in my own life it came as quite a shock being alone. But I know how to stand on my own feet now.'

Quivering with hurt and fury, she proved the point by standing up in one graceful motion.

The anger in his face was replaced by a grim frustration as he looked at her. Georgie was weeping uncontrollably. There was no resistance in her slim body as he gathered her into his arms.

'Things will be fine now.'

Georgie, who didn't feel as if anything would ever be fine, lifted her head. 'How do you figure that?'

He took her chin in his fingers. 'Look at me, *yineka mou*.'

'I don't have much choice, do I?' she returned with a sniff.

'I will learn to be a halfway decent husband.'

His dark eyes lingered on her face and Georgie shifted uneasily. The movement resulted in one of his heavily muscled thighs becoming wedged between her legs. Painfully aware of the lean, hard length of the body so close to her own, she shivered.

'You're serious, aren't you?' It occurred to her that from a distance they would look to passers-by like lovers embracing.

'Deadly serious.' His thumb moved to the full curve of her lush lower lip. Georgie swayed, nailed to the spot by a wave of intense longing.

'This isn't fair,' she whispered.

'I love your mouth. I always did…'

Georgie swallowed hard. 'I don't think my mouth is relevant to this conversation.'

His restless glance continued to move hungrily over her soft features. 'At night I think about your sweet lips on my body and I ache. I ache for you.'

He thought about…he ached for her…! And she ached for him too.

She felt his warm breath touch her sensitive earlobe and sighed, fast losing the fight against the raw urgency that coursed through her pliant body.

Angolos must have sensed her surrender because she could hear the male triumph in his voice as he promised, 'It will be even better than it was when we are together…'

She turned her head and their lips were almost touching when his comment penetrated. With a cry of disgust she pulled away, breathing hard. 'You are such a control freak!' she accused, backing away with her hand pressed to her throat. Her skin felt hot and sticky. 'Well, your tactics won't work this time.'

'Firstly, it wasn't a tactic.'

She focused on his face and saw that there was a damp sheen to his olive-toned skin that made it glisten; the heat in his eyes was fading, leaving a raw frustration in its place.

She decided not to ask what it was. 'And second?'

'Second, it almost worked. Can't you accept that I just want you, and for that matter you want me? It was not part of some sinister plan. I would not take your compliance to mean you'll come back to me. And it's not as though I was about to drag you down onto the sand. It was just a kiss...' His attention shifted to her mouth. '*Almost* a kiss.'

The husky afterthought made her stomach muscles quiver frantically.

Her hands clenched at her sides. '*Angolos...*'

Against all the odds he responded to the anguished appeal in her voice. 'Fine, you want to concentrate on the practical— have you considered the financial aspect of this?'

'What do you mean, "financial"?'

'My son will one day inherit all that I have.'

Her eyes widened; Angolos had a lot! 'I hadn't thought about that...'

'He will be an extremely wealthy man,' he slotted in quietly. 'But he will also inherit responsibilities,' he continued in a matter-of-fact way. 'Wealth and power can be the ruin of some people...I've seen it happen. Nicky will need guidance...not heavy-handed, but loving, parental guidance.'

A stark silence followed his comments.

'You've given me a lot to think about,' she admitted. They were very powerful arguments and she couldn't pretend otherwise.

'Then go away and think...until tomorrow.'

'Tomorrow?' She shook her head. 'That's not long enough,'

she protested. 'I couldn't possibly come to such a major decision so quickly.'

'I'm bending over backwards to be reasonable here, Georgette, but don't push it. Tomorrow.'

Reluctantly she shook her head. 'I should be getting back; Ruth is looking after Nicky.'

'He's a beautiful child.'

Their eyes touched. 'He takes after you.' The moment the unthinking but heartfelt words were out of her mouth she wished she could retract them.

'Georgette, you'll make me blush,' he teased, revealing a set of perfect white teeth as he laughed out loud at her visible discomfiture.

'I'm not telling you anything you don't already know,' she retorted, with as much dignity as she could muster. She had touched his perfection on more than one occasion. Thinking about just how unstinting she had been with her praise made her cringe with embarrassment.

Though, in his favour, for a man who had been endowed with such incredible good looks he really wasn't vain. In fact she had more than once seen him irritated by the attention he got, though mostly he tuned out strangers who gawped.

'Shall I call at the house tomorrow?'

She shook her head. 'Best not.' Tomorrow Dad and Mary were driving Gran back up. 'By the church, about one…'

'I'll be waiting.'

CHAPTER TEN

ACTUALLY he wasn't waiting, she was.

When Georgie arrived there was no sign of Angolos. She might have followed her first cowardly impulse and left if she hadn't known that he would come looking for her.

With a sigh she walked through the gate into the small churchyard. Thoughts far away, she began to wander down the interwoven stone paths past the moss-covered gravestones. Georgie had never found this place at all gloomy, and had often remarked on the tranquil atmosphere.

She stopped, her eyes drawn to a lichen-covered memorial. The weathered inscription in the stone revealed the woman born over three hundred years earlier had had a long life. Georgie's curiosity stirred; had she been happy, this woman born into another century?

There were several wars, an industrial revolution and a sexual revolution separating her from this woman. Her own life was light years away from the one this woman had lived, yet the essentials, the things deep down most people wanted, weren't.

To love and be loved.

'Were you loved...?' Georgie squinted at the worn letters. 'Were you loved, Agnes?' she whispered softly.

If anyone had heard her they would have concluded she was crazy, and maybe, she reflected, they wouldn't be far wrong. She had thought she had been loved; she had discovered that she hadn't been in the cruellest way imaginable.

Georgie turned her back on the gravestone and wished her own past were so easily dismissed.

Eyes closed, she inhaled deeply. It had never crossed her

mind that Angolos wouldn't be as thrilled as she was about her pregnancy. Of course, she hadn't known then what she did now.

Georgie had planned the evening down to the last detail. She'd wanted everything to be perfect, but from the start nothing had gone right.

To begin with the party that Sacha and Olympia had been going to attend had been cancelled at the last minute, so the romantic meal she had planned had become a family affair. Georgie had wanted to scream with frustration, especially when Angolos hadn't turned up.

When he had arrived an hour later than he had promised, he'd seemed distracted and had even been terse with his mother, who had been unwise enough to remonstrate him on his tardiness. Georgie had caught him looking at her so strangely a couple of times that she'd started to think that he had guessed about the baby. That would have accounted for the suppressed tension emanating from him.

The meal had been a stiff, formal affair, but that hadn't been unusual, and had seemed to last for ever. When they had finally retreated to their own suite of rooms she hadn't known what to say. Suddenly her planned speech hadn't seemed right.

Angolos hadn't helped; he'd seemed strangely remote and unapproachable. She had noticed that he had drunk more at dinner than he generally did, and the fine lines bracketing his mouth had suggested he was under some strain.

'Did you have a bad day?' She laid a tentative hand on his arm.

His dark eyes immediately slewed in the direction of the fingers curled lightly over his arm. Though there was no discernible expression on his lean features, Georgie withdrew her hand awkwardly.

His mouth twisted. 'You could say that.'

Hurt and bewildered by the underlying hostility in his manner, she retreated to a chair beside the bed.

She watched as he removed his tie and fell backwards onto the bed. He lay for a moment spread-eagled with his eyes closed. Then from his prone position he began to unfasten the buttons of his shirt.

The action revealed the golden skin of lean-muscled torso and Georgie's breath snagged in her throat. He was simply stunningly beautiful.

He looked at her through heavy-lidded, half-closed eyes.

'You were quiet tonight,' he observed.

'Was I?' *What would he say when she told him?* She glanced wistfully towards the open double doors that led out to the balcony and adopted a coaxing tone. 'Why don't we sit outside? I love to look at the moonlight on the sea.' And what could be a more romantic spot to tell him her news?

'You sound like a tourist.' Before she had an opportunity to respond to his dismissive comment he added thickly, 'And anyway, I prefer to look at you. You look particularly glowing this evening.'

'Do I?'

'Yes.' His long fingers closed around her wrist. 'Tell me what you've been doing with yourself today. Have you missed me?'

Only every other second. 'I've been pretty busy, actually.' She had taken his recent hints about being more self-reliant to heart.

She didn't want to become a clingy wife. It had helped that Alan had come over and had been staying in the nearby village with his friend.

Georgie willingly responded to the gentle tug on her arm and fell in a happy heap beside him. She flipped over onto her tummy and, with her chin propped in her hands, smiled at him. He didn't smile back. 'Alan went home today.'

'How sad.'

'Don't be mean about him,' she begged.

'*Mean…?*'

'Well, you're—' She gasped as he turned her wrist over and pressed his lips to the pale-skinned inner aspect; she shivered as all the fine hairs on her body stood on end.

'Have I ever told you that you're the most beautiful man that ever drew breath?'

'Not recently.'

His husky velvet voice sent a shiver along her hopelessly sensitive nerve endings. 'I suppose I have been a bit moody lately,' she admitted. When he realised why, she hoped he would forgive her recent crankiness and mood swings. 'I didn't know why myself until today.'

'Are you going to let me in on the secret?'

'Soon,' she promised as with her best enigmatic smile she hitched up her long skirts to her waist and straddled his body.

'What are you doing?'

'I'm just doing,' she told him primly, 'what any dutiful wife would.' She frowned as she concentrated on slipping the remaining buttons of his shirt. Within seconds she had exposed all of his lean, hard torso. She ran her fingertips over the silky, hair-roughened surface and felt his stomach muscles contract. His skin was like oiled silk. She gave a voluptuous sigh of pleasure.

His hands tightened possessively over the smooth, bare skin of her thighs. 'What has brought this on?'

'Don't you like it?'

'Oh, I like it. I'm just wondering why you should decide to take the initiative tonight…'

Did that mean he found her unadventurous and boring in bed? The thought took the edge off her pleasure and dented her newly discovered confidence.

'Tonight's special.'

'I think you'll remember it.'

Georgie, rehearsing what she was going to say in her head,

barely registered his cryptic response. 'Angolos, I've got something to tell you.' She leaned forward, her eyes glowing with anticipation, her cheeks gently flushed. With a grunt of irritation she pinned the strands of her hair that brushed his face behind one ear. 'Sorry.'

'I like your hair on my skin. It feels...' He closed his eyes and muttered something angry in Greek under his breath.

'I think what I've got to say will cheer you up.'

Considering what had followed, that was probably the silliest comment she had ever made, Georgie reflected grimly.

'You're going to be a father, Angolos. I'm going to have a baby.'

His eyes stayed closed—she began to think he'd not heard her—then, dark, deep and impenetrable, they flickered open.

'Pregnant?'

She nodded, and experienced the first stirrings of fear. Something was badly wrong, but she had no idea what... Perhaps he felt it was too soon, which didn't make sense because he was the one who had just shrugged when she had mentioned precautions...

'I know we weren't trying...and we didn't discuss it, but I thought you might be happy. You are happy?'

'Happy? I'm bloody delirious,' he contended grimly. 'Can't you tell, *yineka mou*?'

'I d...don't understand...' she stuttered.

Angolos rounded a corner in the lane and stopped. He could see her sitting on the wall, oblivious for the moment to his presence. He took the opportunity to study her undetected.

With her hair tied back in a pony-tail and her face innocent of make-up she looked more like a teenager than the mother of a child—*his* child. The idea still seemed strange to him. Strange as in bordering on miraculous, though he didn't expect Georgie to share his sense of wonder.

'You were far away.'

Georgie jumped at the sound of his voice. 'You're late.'

He didn't react to her shrill, accusatory tone. 'Have you come to a decision?'

'I have.' She had thought long and hard; she had thought until her brain felt as if it would explode.

One dark brow lifted. The casual observer, looking at his face, would have said her reply was in no way important to Angolos. But Georgie was not a casual observer; she knew that Angolos cared very badly about her reply.

'And...?' The muscle in his tense jaw continued to click steadily as he held her eyes.

Not into playing games, she replied immediately. 'I agree that I have no right to deny Nicky his heritage. I can protect him now, but I won't be able to always. I'll just have to teach him to look after himself. I think you'd be good at that, Angolos. So I will come to Greece with you, on trial basis.'

She saw the muscles of his shoulders relax. 'Thank you for that, Georgette. For my part I swear that I will do my best not to disappoint you.'

The palpable sincerity in his voice brought an emotional lump to her throat. 'I don't think you would, but you didn't let me finish. There are conditions.'

'Whatever you say,' he said immediately.

'Don't you think you ought to hear what they are first?' she asked him.

'Bring on your demands. It doesn't matter what they are. I will do anything it takes to develop a relationship with my son.'

'I understand that.'

One dark brow arched in sardonic enquiry as he scanned her face. 'But you have your doubts? You don't think it will work out?'

This drew a reluctant laugh from her. 'Only a couple of thousand.' Her expression sobered as she lifted her face to his; she could almost feel his impatience. 'It didn't work last time.' Feeling her control slipping, she turned and began to walk towards the church.

Angolos cursed softly under his breath as he fell into step beside her. 'The situation isn't the same.'

That much was true. Last time he had loved her, or professed to at least. This time there was no pretence that his feelings for her were what they once had been; this was all about wanting to be a father to his son.

'I know that, but everything else is. You…' She stopped and smiled at an elderly couple who walked past hand in hand.

'Lovely afternoon.'

'Marvellous,' she agreed.

'Why are the British obsessed with the weather?' Before she could defend the national obsession he added, 'Why are you determined to be negative about this?'

'I'm not being negative,' she protested. 'I'm being realistic. We're going back to the same house. You're the same man, your mother will still resent me.'

'My mother did not resent you!'

Georgie smiled and looked away. 'If you say so.'

'Perhaps you have left out the most significant obstacle.'

She paused and ran her fingers along the moss-covered wall beside the church gate. Her glance lifted to the tiny church with its square Norman tower. As a young girl she had spent many an afternoon imagining herself walking up the aisle here, and standing underneath the big horse chestnut having her picture taken in its shade.

The reality could not have been more different: an anonymous register office. Angolos had let it be known that he hadn't actually wanted a big wedding. 'Been there, done that…but, of course, if you want…?' he added.

'No, I hate big weddings,' she lied dutifully. 'It's the next twenty years that counts, not the day itself.'

He laughed at her earnestness and called her a hopeless romantic, but she was happy because she had pleased him.

With a sigh she rested her back against the wall now. 'And what is that?' She stretched out her hand and languidly watched the dappled light play across her skin.

'You're still the same person too.'

She shook her head, but didn't look at him. 'You're wrong, Angolos. I'm not the same person at all.'

'You mean you won't grow discontented this time.'

This time she did look up. *'Discontented…?'*

'You never made any effort to fit in.'

'Fit in!' she exclaimed in heated response to this monumentally unfair claim. 'Short of changing my identity, that was never going to happen.'

'What are you talking about?'

As if he didn't know.

'Tell me, Angolos,' she began with vibrating antagonism. 'How long had we been married before you began regretting it? A week…two…?' *Now* he was prepared to put his life on hold to be with their son; back then he hadn't even been able to free a weekend to spend time with her! If her friend Alan hadn't arrived she would have felt even lonelier.

'This,' he said heavily, 'is getting us nowhere.'

'Maybe someone is trying to tell us something,' she murmured as she levered herself up onto the wall.

'It's not exactly constructive raking up the past every five seconds.' Angolos's gaze moved from the small hands folded primly in her lap to her neatly crossed ankles and his jaw clenched.

'You look like a child,' he accused throatily.

She continued banging her heels against the stone as he set his hands against the uneven wall either side of her. But it was an uphill battle to continue to act as if her pulses weren't racing like crazy and she weren't painfully aware of the proximity of his warm male body.

'I'm not, and I've got the stretch marks to prove it.' Without thinking, she moved her hand to hover above the area low on her belly, where the silvery lines were a permanent reminder of her motherhood.

'I'm well aware you're not a child.' He exhaled a long shuddering breath that sucked in the muscles of his flat belly and expanded his impressive chest. He dragged a hand through his dark hair. 'I used to know your body as well as I knew my own.'

The accusing throaty addition brought her startled glance to his face. Their eyes meshed and her insides dissolved.

'The attraction is still there.'

'I don't know if Greece fell short of your expectations or I did? But it is my home and once,' he added, 'it was yours. I would like for my son to have the opportunity to learn to love it also.'

'It was never my home.' The sadness in her eyes was tinged with resentment. 'I was always a visitor and not a welcome one at that.' His mother, the daunting Olympia, had made sure of that.

'That's ludicrous. This melodrama isn't helping anyone,' he retorted impatiently.

Georgie didn't respond. She knew perfectly well that he would never believe that his family had loathed her; in front of him they had been sweetness and light.

'I don't want to share a home with your mother and sister.'

'Is that a fact?'

She could tell from his expression that he didn't take her seriously. She took a deep breath. If she was going to do this, she was going to do it on her terms. 'Let me rephrase that. I *won't* share a house with your mother and sister.'

Eyes narrowed, he scanned her face. 'You're serious?'

'Deadly serious.'

His expression changed. 'You expect me to throw my mother and sister from their home?'

Georgie could see he was totally outraged by her suggestion. 'They're hardly going to be homeless, are they?' His mother owned a palatial villa a few miles away and a town house in Athens and they were only the ones Georgie knew about! 'As for Sacha, if you let her stand on her own feet instead of fighting her battles…'

'She got married last year.'

'Oh, that's great.'

'They had a falling out and—'

'Let me guess—she came back home.'

Angolos's expression grew defensive. 'And why should she not?'

'Hasn't it ever occurred to you that she's never going to sort out her own problems while she knows you're always going to ride to the rescue when the going gets tough?'

His eyes narrowed. 'Do you dislike my family so much?'

She released an exasperated sigh. 'I don't dislike them at all,' she protested. 'They're not keen on me. Actually I think they'd dislike anyone who wasn't Sonia.'

'That's nonsense.'

She felt her anger mount at his dismissive attitude. 'They still think you'll get back together.'

'That is totally ridiculous. We divorced years ago. Who knows why we ever got married…?' he added half to himself.

Angolos knew from personal experience that youthful infatuation might feel intense, but was by nature a transitory thing doomed to fade as the people involved matured. Maybe it was the fact he and Sonia had both wanted out of the relationship that they had remained friends—whatever the reason, the civilised arrangement owed more to luck than good judgement.

'It could have something to do with the fact she's beautiful, talented, sexy and can't keep her hands off you.'

'Were you jealous?'

Georgie laughed. She couldn't help it, he sounded so startled. 'You really are not the sharpest knife in the drawer, are you? Of *course* I was jealous. What wife wouldn't be?'

'One that did not have a self-esteem issue.'

When he got that smug, self-satisfied look she wanted to hit him. 'Your ex-wife told me I was just the sort of quiet, homely wife you needed.'

'Sonia didn't mean anything by it, I'm sure. She just says the first thing that comes into her head. She's very spontaneous.'

The speed with which he flew to the other woman's defence brought a bitter smile to her lips. If he had been half as eager to defend me... She pushed aside the unfinished thought and squared her jaw.

'If I asked the staff to do anything they checked first with your mother before.'

'Ridiculous.'

'It was ridiculous that I put up with it, but I was very young and naïve.' The observation made him flinch, but Georgie was too caught up in her own recollections to notice. 'That was bad enough,' she recalled, 'but when they automatically deferred to Sonia as well I felt as if I was a poor relation... No, that's not right, I didn't feel as though I was a relation at all.' She swallowed and gave a grim smile.

'You're exaggerating.' Despite this claim, she saw for the first time a flicker of uncertainty in his eyes.

'How would you know? You were never there.'

'I had been away from work for a long time. I had a lot of catching up to do and my mother went out of her way to make you feel at home,' he told her stiffly.

Sure she did, Georgie thought as she tactfully conceded the point with an inclination of her head.

Angolos's face was a rigid mask of constraint as he replied. 'If I had wanted Sonia I would have stayed married to her. I wanted you.'

Georgie's stomach flipped. Her covert glance at his hard,

male, deliciously streamlined body resulted in an adrenaline surge of huge proportions. She inhaled deeply and nearly fell off the wall.

'And you wanted me…' Her heart was hammering so fast she could barely breathe. Her knees had acquired the consistency of cotton wool.

'And you wanted me.' He said it again.

A scared sound rasped in her throat and her eyes lifted. 'Things change,' she croaked defiantly.

Angolos studied her flushed face, lingering on the softness of her trembling lips. 'And some things don't.'

Silently she shook her head.

He took her chin in his hand and tilted her face up to him. There was anger in the dark eyes that moved hungrily over her delicate features. 'Why can't you admit it?' he rasped.

'Because I don't want to feel this way…when you…' Without warning she slid off the wall and under his restraining arm. Eyes blazing, her breasts heaving, she stood defiantly glaring at him.

'I'm not an impressionable kid. Getting me into bed won't change my mind.'

'It might make you feel less frustrated, however.' Georgie was about to respond angrily to this supremely arrogant suggestion, when he added, 'I know it would make me feel less frustrated. Where you are concerned I've never had any self-control…' He watched her eyes widen with shock and his lips twisted in a self-derisive smile. 'You haven't the faintest idea what it does to me to be this close to you and not touch…' he said thickly.

A surge of heat travelled through her body. *'Tell me…'* she demanded throatily, then almost immediately started to backtrack as though her life depended on it. 'No…no, I didn't mean that.'

He responded to her denial with a disturbing smile. 'Are you sure?' His smouldering glance dropped to her parted lips.

Georgie heard a soft moan and realised with a sense of shock that she had made it. Ashamed of the desire that drenched her shaking body in a wave of intense sexual heat, she tried to turn away, but her knees gave and she stumbled.

His arm shot out to steady her. Heads close together, their eyes meshed. 'Do you like the idea of me wanting to touch you, Georgette?'

An image of the last time they'd made love flashed into her head. He had walked into the bedroom and she hadn't heard him. She hadn't known he was there until she'd turned around and found him standing with his shoulders against the door-frame, staring at her.

He'd looked so immaculate in an open-necked shirt and tailored trousers that she'd immediately wished that she had not delayed taking her shower. 'How long have you been there?' He didn't reply, just carried on looking at her. 'I was clearing out the drawers of this—'

He levered himself off the door and moved unhurriedly towards her, tall, lean and shockingly sexy. 'There are people to do that sort of things.'

He reached her side in seconds, and since his eyes had locked onto hers his unwavering stare had not left her face for an instant.

'I keep forge—'

The rest of her sentence remained unspoken as he bent forward and, taking her face between his hands, he fitted his mouth to hers. He kissed her with a driving desperation that bent her body backwards. She clung to him, shaking violently with need. She gasped and moaned his name as his hands slid under her skirt, pushing back the lace of her pants to touch the damp heat between her legs.

'Whenever I touch you, you are ready for me...'

'*Georgette...?*'

The sound of Angolos's voice dragged her back to the present. Disorientated, she blinked.

'Are you all right?'

'You asked me if I liked the idea of you wanting to touch me…?'

The dark colour scoring his high cheekbones deepened. 'You're right. This isn't the place or time—'

'Thinking is good, doing is better.'

And Angolos had been very good at *doing*. When she closed her eyes she could see him above her, his skin glistening as he drove deep into her again and again. Her cries urging him on and on.

With a frightened gasp she opened her eyes. *'What am I doing?'*

He caught hold of her chin and angled her face up to his. 'I don't know, but if you don't stop doing it I could end up getting arrested.' His eyes gleamed with laughter but, under the laughter, darker, more dangerous emotions lurked. The darkness in his eyes exerted a powerful fascination for her. It always had.

As she lowered her mortified gaze she caught sight of a bead of sweat running down the brown column of his throat. She followed its progress, unable to tear her eyes from it.

'I didn't mean to.' She gave a self-condemnatory groan. 'That sounds so stupid! But I just do and say things around you that I wouldn't even think around anyone else… I'm really sorry.'

'Do I look offended?'

Her eyes lifted. She shook her head and restlessly twisted her hair into a knot on the nape of her neck.

Don't even think about telling him how he looks, she cautioned herself.

'You still want me. This is not to my mind a cause for repentance.'

'Well, there's no need to act as if you didn't already know,' she returned, centring her cross frown on his dark, devastatingly handsome face.

'I didn't consider it the foregone conclusion you seem to,' he contended drily.

His eyes strayed to the exposed length of her slender throat and stayed there. Flushing, she let her hair fall and lowered her arms. Crossing them in front of her chest, oblivious to the fact the protective action pushed her compressed breasts upwards, she pursed her lips in a scornful grimace.

'I bet you were a bundle of insecurity.' Angolos, a victim to fragile self-esteem...? Oh, sure, that was *really* likely.

'The flame that burns brightest does not always last the longest. You were very young—'

'And stupid,' she cut in angrily. 'Yes, a lot of people think that, and it just goes to show that a few more years on the clock don't necessarily make you any less stupid!' If anything she wanted him more now than she had then.

'So that aspect of being back with me does not fill you with disgust?'

'The sex was always pretty fantastic,' she grunted, avoiding his eyes as though her life depended on it. 'It was the other stuff we were terrible at.'

'So, we will work on the "other stuff", and enjoy the sex,' he announced, sounding pleased with himself, which, considering she had just told him she fancied the pants off him, was not surprising. Why *did* her mouth detach itself from her brain when she was around this man?

'That remains to be seen,' she replied as he fell in step beside her, moderating his long stride to match hers.

'Where are we going?'

'I'm going to pick up Nicky from Ruth's, and then—'

'I'll come with you.'

CHAPTER ELEVEN

GEORGIE walked into a room full of people and blinked.

'Look at her,' Robert Kemp teased. 'She forgot we were coming.' He enfolded his startled daughter in a bear hug.

'No, of course I didn't, Dad,' Georgie lied. 'How are you?'

'We're fine...but never mind us. How's my favourite grandson? More to the point, *where's* my favourite grandson?' he asked, looking around the room expectantly.

Her more-observant stepmother laid a concerned hand on Georgie's arm. 'Is anything wrong, Georgie, dear?'

'I'm fine, thanks, Mary. He's in the garden, Dad.' On cue the sound of Nicky's high-pitched laughter drifted in through the open door. 'No, don't go yet,' she added, catching her father's arm as he headed towards the French door. 'I need to tell you something.' *Deep breath...keep calm, be firm...don't get apologetic.* 'No, actually I need to tell *everyone* something,' she corrected.

'Well, go on, then, don't keep us in suspense,' her father urged impatiently.

'Sit down, Robert,' his wife, her eyes on Georgie's tense figure, instructed sharply. 'Can't you see there's something wrong?'

'There's nothing *wrong* exactly, I've just made a decision.'

Her grandmother spoke for the first time. 'It's that man, isn't it? You've seen him again. Oh, yes, and I've heard that he's been here. You can't drive around in a flashy car like his and not get noticed.'

'What man?' Robert Kemp demanded in exasperation. 'Will someone please tell me what's going on?'

'The Constantine creature.'

112

Robert turned to his daughter, his face stern. 'Tell me this isn't true, Georgie.'

Georgie scanned the three faces staring accusingly at her. No wonder I feel as if I'm on trial, she thought wearily. 'Angolos has a right to see Nicky, Dad.'

Her father groaned and clutched his head in his hands. 'He's sucked you in again, hasn't he? That man has caused this family nothing but heartache since the moment he appeared and I for one wish you'd never laid eyes on him.'

'Well, if I hadn't I wouldn't have Nicky, would I?'

'Don't be smart with me, my girl. I hope you've told him we don't need him.'

'Not exactly,' Georgie admitted uneasily. 'Actually,' she added, 'I agreed to go back to Greece with him...'

There was a stunned silence.

Her father was the first to recover his voice. He jerked his head towards the window. 'Is he here now?'

'Dad, please...?' Georgie begged.

'Were you born stupid?' he wanted to know.

Her grandmother reached for her pillbox and popped a pill with her hand pressed significantly to her heart. 'If that man suggested you jump into the nearest lake you would.' There was nothing frail about her contemptuous observation. 'All he has to do is get you into bed and you'd sell your own soul or, in this case,' she declared dramatically, 'your son.'

Georgie flushed at the accusation. 'Nicky has a right to know his father, Gran.' *Does he? Didn't he lose those rights...?*

'This isn't about Nicky, it's about you,' the old lady retorted.

Georgie coloured guiltily. This was a charge she had levelled at herself. And she still couldn't swear, hand on heart, that there wasn't an element of truth in it. She wanted to do the right thing for Nicky, but, when the *right thing* involved being back with the man who was the passion of her life, could she ever be sure her decision was totally objective?

'If that man goes near my grandson I'll…' Robert added.

Georgie lost her patience. Her family had been there when she'd needed them, but this was her life they were discussing.

'You'll what, Dad?' she asked. 'Teach him a lesson? Do you really think you could? Sorry.' She bit her lip. 'I shouldn't have said that. I know you have my interests at heart, but this is my life. This isn't an impulse, you know. I've given it a lot of thought.'

'Well, in that case there's no more to be said.'

Georgie heaved a sigh of relief. 'Thank you, Dad. I really appreciate this.'

Robert looked at the hand extended to him and deliberately ignored it as he walked to his wife's side and placed an arm around her shoulder. 'You go to Greece with your so-called husband if that is what you want, but if you do you are no longer my daughter.'

'You can't mean that, Dad,' she said, even though she knew he did.

'Robert!' her stepmother protested. 'You can't make her choose this way… He doesn't mean it, Georgie, dear.'

'I do mean it. You go to Greece and I wash my hands of you.' He patted his wife's hand. 'Sometimes tough love is called for, Mary. This is a matter of loyalty.' Face set in stone, he turned to his daughter. 'What is it to be, Georgie? Your family or this man who cares so much about his son that he's been too busy for the last three years to notice he's alive?'

'I've made my decision, Dad.'

An expression of blank amazement spread across Robert Kemp's florid face. 'You're going to Greece?'

Her grandmother, who had been watching proceedings from her armchair, reached for her walking stick and rose majestically to her feet. 'You ungrateful child.'

'Please, Gran…' She slid an anguished look in her father's

direction. 'I know what it's like not to see a parent. I don't want Nicky—'

'You think your father stopped your mother seeing you?'

'I don't blame Dad. I know Mum hurt him badly.'

'Your father is too soft to tell you. He didn't. The fact is she didn't want to. My daughter-in-law didn't care about you at all,' the old lady spat contemptuously. 'The only thing she cared about was her pretty-boy waiter and he didn't want a baby. I think,' she added, her normal strong voice quivering, 'this could be called history repeating itself.'

Shock had drained the colour from Georgie's face. Her eyes darted from one person to the other without really seeing them. Silly, really. She knew that if her mother had wanted to contact her she would have, but like any child she had nursed her fantasies. And those images had persisted into adulthood: her mother a victim of cruel fate, separated against her will from the daughter she loved.

'I wouldn't leave Nicky, not ever, not for anything.'

'Of course you wouldn't, Georgie,' her stepmother soothed. 'You're a marvellous mother.'

'I couldn't agree more.' Angolos waited until every eye in the room was fixed on him before continuing. 'Georgette has been doing the job of two parents for three years. I think it's time she was relieved of some of the load.'

Georgie turned towards the sound of that deep, confident voice. She experienced a wave of inexpressible relief as their eyes connected.

'Angolos, I…' How much had he heard?

'I think this young man needs a clean-up.' Acting as if there weren't an atmosphere you could cut with a knife in the room, Angolos slanted an amused look at the grubby figure in his arms. The love in his face was so palpable that Georgie couldn't believe she was the only one who could see it.

That was why she was doing this.

Angolos shared his smile between the three other occupants of the room. 'I will wait here.'

'I don't think that's such a good idea,' Georgie said dubiously as he transferred their restless son to her arms.

'You've got him?'

She nodded. 'I think it might be better if you just went. You can ring me later.' He simply couldn't be oblivious to the hostility aimed at him, but from his manner you'd never have known it.

Her father, apparently sharing her view, muttered under his breath, 'He's got a nerve.'

'You haven't changed a jot, Robert—are you working out?' While the other man pressed a hand to his expanding middle and turned dark red with incoherent rage, Angolos turned calmly to Georgie. 'Go on,' he urged. 'It will be fine.'

Throwing a last worried frown over her shoulder Georgie mounted the staircase.

Angolos's smile lasted until he heard the sound of a door opening and closing upstairs. 'Right, you can't stand the sight of me—I can live with that. I have an incredibly thick skin and I am not at all sensitive,' he admitted. 'The only person your insults hurt is Georgette and I don't actually think you want to do that…?' He arched a dark brow and levelled a questioning look at his father-in-law, who glared at him with venomous dislike.

'In your place,' Angolos admitted, 'I would probably feel the same way. You would like me to disappear from your lives. It isn't going to happen, so I suggest you get used to it.'

'*Never!*' Robert Kemp grunted.

'I have no particular fondness for you either, but I am prepared to tolerate you for Georgette's sake. You are my son's grandparents and I hope you will remain an important part of his life. I realise that you spoke in the heat of the moment and you have no wish to disown your daughter or grandson, so I think it will be best all around if we forget you ever said it.'

'You…*you* think…?' Robert blustered, ignoring his wife's agonised aside to leave it be. 'What makes you think I give a damn what you think?'

'I don't. But I think you care about what Georgette thinks. Perhaps we should concentrate on what we have in common.'

'And what would that be?' Robert sneered.

'We both want Georgette to be happy. I can make her happy.' With that he walked out of the room leaving a stunned silence behind him.

Though his approach had been silent Georgie sensed his presence at her shoulder. 'He fell asleep.'

'So I see,' Angolos said, looking at the sleeping child. 'Amazing,' he breathed softly. 'How are you?' he added, not taking his eyes from Nicky's cherubic face.

'As well as could be expected considering my family have cast me off.' Despite the tough words, he could feel the waves of hurt emanating from her.

'And that would bother you…?'

Narrow shoulders hunched, she picked up a stuffed toy from the floor and tucked it in beside the sleeping child. 'Do one thing for me,' she husked, not turning around.

'It's possible I might do one thing for you.'

'Please don't be nice,' she pleaded from between clenched teeth.

His expressive lips quirked. 'You want me to be unpleasant?'

'I want you to be yourself, which amounts to much the same thing.'

'I will do my best to behave with the callous lack of consideration you expect of me.'

Georgie whipped around and promptly forgot the acid retort that had hovered on the tip of her tongue. He was closer than she had anticipated...*very much closer*. Close enough to feel the heat rising off his skin, smell the warm, male, musky scent of him. She couldn't summon the strength to fight as she felt herself sink beneath a wave of enervating lust.

'I only want you to hold me because I'm temporarily feeling alone and sorry for myself.' *Did I really say that out loud?*

Angolos cupped her face between his big hands. 'You're not alone,' he rasped.

Yes, I said it! 'I'm not normally a needy person,' she promised, feeling weak tears squeeze out from her closed eyelids. 'I just need a tissue and possibly a drink.'

Something flickered in his deep-set eyes. 'But not me?'

'I make mistakes,' she told him. 'But not twice,' she added grimly as she pulled back from him, back in control—or as much as she ever was around him—of her feelings.

His expression hardened. 'I will make the flight arrangements and contact you with the details. I'm assuming you don't travel light with a child?'

'What flight arrangements?'

He looked irritated. 'What flight arrangements do you think I mean? I will fly over later tonight and organise things that end, then—'

'You think I'm going to drop everything and leave immediately?'

'Not immediately, but I see no reason to delay.'

She stared at him incredulously. 'No, of course you don't.' *How could I have forgotten how selfish and single-minded he is...?*

He shook his head and sat down on the bed. Something she immediately wished he hadn't done. 'What is your problem? I have acceded to all your demands, placated your family... Do not push your luck, Georgette,' he advised.

'Oh, the "I'll do anything to be with my son" didn't last very long, did it?' she observed with withering scorn. 'I have commitments here.'

Angolos's facial muscles clenched, giving his face the appearance of stone as he asked in a voice devoid of all emotion, 'Does he know you are married?'

Georgie shook her head, frowning. '*He…?* Will you stop talking in riddles…?' Then as his meaning hit her angry heat flooded her face! 'I don't believe you! Do you really think I'd be stupid enough to commit to another man? After you!' she stressed.

'You don't have a boyfriend.' He sounded cautious, but not unhappy with this information. 'Then what commitments are we talking about?'

'I have a job, I'm contractually obliged to give the school notice and even if I wasn't I wouldn't dream of leaving them in the lurch.' She made a quick mental assessment. 'I won't be able to leave until half-term at the earliest.'

'And when is half-term?'

'The end of October.'

'That is not acceptable.'

She shrugged and thrust her hands in the pockets of her jeans. *'Tough.'*

'You really have changed.'

'I'll take that as a compliment.'

'I'm sure I would be able to get the school to release you immediately.'

Georgie had no doubt he could, though he would probably delegate the task. 'And I suppose that would involve throwing sacks full of money at them.' Sometimes the Constantine name was enough.

'Not *sacks* full.'

'Typical!'

The way he was looking at her made it obvious he was totally mystified by her anger. 'Don't take that "I'm being reasonable and you're being irrational" tone with me; I always hated it!' she told him.

'Thank you for sharing that with me.'

'I'm not your sister. I don't want, or need, you to make my problems go away by producing your cheque-book. Besides, this time I'm not burning my bridges. If things don't work out I'm going to need a reference.'

'To anticipate failure is hardly a positive attitude.'

'Maybe not, but it's a practical one,' she said, responding to his criticism with a careless shrug. 'I'm a mother now. I can't act on a whim—I have to consider the consequences of my actions.'

'And you married me on a whim—is that what you're saying?'

Her mouth twisted in a cynical smile of self-derision. 'I like to think of it more as temporary insanity.'

Oblivious to the fact that her confidence had caused Angolos to stiffen, she took the top item on a pile of freshly laundered clothes waiting to be put away and began to fold it with geometric precision. The mundane action helped steady her nerves.

'It's a pity really we didn't just have sex as my dad suggested.'

'Your father told you to sleep with me?'

His outraged tone brought her head up and she found herself looking into eyes that had narrowed into icy, incredulous slits.

'Well, wouldn't you prefer your daughter to sleep with the wrong man rather than marry him?' she charged impatiently.

'If my daughter was involved with the wrong man I would not advise her to have sex with him,' he assured her grimly.

'What would you do?' she asked, even though she could hazard a guess from his expression.

'I would remove the man from her life.'

'And if he didn't want to go?'

He looked astonished that she needed to ask. 'I would not give him a choice.'

She shook her head. 'I think it's just as well that Nicky wasn't a girl.'

'Our next child might be, though.'

The colour drained from her face. 'What did you say?' she choked.

His brows lifted. 'Would you condemn Nicky to be an only child?' he wanted to know.

'*Me condemn…!* You really are a piece of work. Don't you *dare* try and use moral blackmail on me.'

'Moral blackmail.'

'Don't give me that innocent look. I've seen wolves who looked more innocent than you.'

The accusation drew a grin from him. 'I believe that wolves suffer from a very bad press. They are not the bad guys of popular fiction. Did you know they mate for life?' he asked.

'I'm willing to give wolves the benefit of the doubt,' she gritted. 'But we both know that you'd do whatever it took to get what you wanted.'

'*You* don't want another baby?' Despite his mild tone his eyes were fixed with a curious intensity on her face.

She blinked; the question took her aback. Did she want another baby? 'That's not the point—'

'I would say it's very much the point,' he inserted drily.

'It's far too early…' She stopped and angled a searching look at his lean face. 'Do *you* want a baby?'

'And if I said I did, would it make a difference to you?'

She looked from the sensual curve of his mouth to the velvety darkness of his eyes and felt her concentration slipping… Her expression hardened.

'You expect me to believe you give a damn about what I think?' She released a scornful trill of laughter and saw the anger flicker in his liquid dark eyes. 'Let's not drift into fantasy land here…'

Angolos cut across her. 'Actually I don't feel that having a baby at this time would be a sensible idea.'

The colour in her cheeks receded. She ought to welcome his comment, she told herself crossly. Anyone would think I *wanted* to have his baby. 'When we don't even know if we'll be together in two weeks' time, let alone two years, I couldn't agree more,' she contended coolly.

'The positive attitude again. You know, Georgette, cynical doesn't suit you.'

'Get used to it, Angolos,' she suggested, maintaining her indifferent pose.

'Do you realise that the moment I start to get close to you…' He took an actual step towards her and without thinking Georgie retreated two steps. 'I was going to say, you push me away, but maybe that should have been you run away.'

A defiant frown formed on her face as she met his ironic smile. 'I'm really not in the mood for your silly games.'

'I'm not playing games, Georgette. I know you want to punish me,' he revealed in a harsh voice, 'but hasn't it occurred to you that I'm not the only one suffering here? You're hurting too. You want me, Georgette. We both know that.'

She opened her mouth to angrily rebut this claim and stopped. She released a long, slow, shuddering breath. 'I am hurting, but there's not a lot I can do about it. And I doubt very much if getting into your bed is going to make that hurt go away. I will probably sleep with you, Angolos.' She saw triumph flare in his eyes and added with a self-derisive shrug, 'You're right—I have very little self-control where you are concerned. But I can't let myself trust you again, Angolos; you hurt me so much.'

The taut silence lengthened. Angolos walked over to the window. 'That cuts both ways.'

Bewildered, she stared at his broad back. 'I hurt you…?'

Angolos turned back; he didn't want to hear another denial. 'I really think there is no point dissecting what went wrong between us.'

On one level he could recognise how the situation could

have driven her into another man's arms: she had felt isolated; he had been too busy with work to give her the attention she needed...recognise but never forgive.

'I thought you wanted to talk,' she protested, bewildered by his swift change of mood.

'I think we should talk about the future.'

'Suits me.' She shot him a wary glance. 'But let's not go over ground we've already covered,' she cautioned.

'What ground would that be?'

'Babies,' she elaborated.

'I was not...I actually think you're a marvellous mother.'

Georgie's eyes widened. Coming from Angolos, who didn't throw around the compliments, this was praise indeed. 'I'm a fairly all right mother,' she corrected. 'I'm a long way from marvellous. I make loads of mistakes. I expect you will too. It's a steep learning curve so don't expect to get it right the first time. I suppose it's not unlike riding a bike or...'

'*Or?*'

'I forget,' she said, unable to think on the spur of the moment of a more convincing lie. Angolos didn't look convinced.

She released a hiss of angry frustration and she shot him a look of fulminating frustration. 'I was going to say making love, but I'm sure you were always perfect at that, *damn you!*' she added with a resentful sniff.

The look of astonishment that spread across his face was swiftly supplanted by a slow, sensual smile. 'There's no need to look so smug.'

'I don't feel smug. I'd just forgotten how much you always made me laugh.' Then to her dismay he did just that in a loud and uninhibited way.

Hell, she thought, he really did have the sexiest laugh in the world.

'Shut up,' she hissed, 'Nicky will wake up, or someone will come up to see what's going on.'

'Is this better?' he asked.

Georgie studied the sober face he showed her. 'Your hair's sticking up,' she said. It wasn't, but it helped her not say what she wanted to. *You're beautiful* might take this conversation in a direction she really didn't want to go!

'Thanks,' he said, drawing a hand over the neatly trimmed pelt. 'Has your family got something against laughter?'

'No, just you.' The rueful smile created a brief sense of unity. 'Do you remember…?' she began, then stopped.

'What?' he prompted.

'I was just thinking about the first time you met the family, and your face when Gran asked you if you worked in a bar. You looked so astonished.' She shook her head. The memory of his aghast expression was so strong that it was hard to keep the quiver of amusement from her voice. 'And you said no, but you thought that you might own a vineyard, but you'd have to ch…check.'

'I did check and I own two, but they are very small.'

CHAPTER TWELVE

'YOU'LL wake him,' Georgie reproached Angolos again before stuffing her fist on her mouth to stifle her own laughter. She laughed until her ribs ached and when she stopped she wiped away the tears from her cheeks. A quick peek revealed that Nicky was still sound asleep.

'It's lucky he's a...' She turned towards Angolos and promptly forgot what she had been about to say.

There was no lingering amusement on his face. Under the sweep of his dark, luxuriant lashes his eyes glittered. The expression on his lean face was intense and raw.

The air between them suddenly buzzed with an almost visible electric charge. It made the fine hairs on her arms stand on end and caused a tell-tale, quivery ache low in her belly.

If she didn't do something and do it quick things were going to happen. And she didn't want that, *did she*?

'You're staring,' she accused with a weak little laugh that fooled nobody, especially herself.

He carried on staring.

She looked at his mouth, seeing it against her breasts. Inside her shirt her nipples grew hard as though his lips had actually brushed over them.

'This is a trial,' she began, calling on every ounce of her will-power to control her voice. 'I was explaining, before you hijacked the conversation, that I'm going to give work my notice.'

There was a long uncomfortable silence while he studied the rigid lines of her determined face.

'They've always been good to me at the school. Nicky has a free place at the nursery,' she continued.

'So it's non-negotiable?'

Her shoulders sagged in relief. 'Yes.'

'In that case I suppose I'd better rearrange my schedule.'

Georgie, who had been expecting something along the lines of, *Over my dead body,* raised suspicious eyes to his face. 'What do you mean?'

'I mean that now that I've found my son I'm not about to wait to be his father. I will relocate.'

'But your work!' she protested.

He dismissed his multimillion-pound company with a casual shrug of his shoulders. 'If necessary I will work from home.'

'Don't be ridiculous. You don't even know where I work and you can't possibly run an international company from a Sussex village.'

He gave her a mocking look. 'Anyone would think you didn't want me to move in with you, *yineka mou,*' he drawled.

Anyone would be right. Her body grew rigid as the full import of his comment penetrated. *'Move in…?'* She echoed sharply.

'I think we should start as we mean to go on. This is to be a marriage in every sense of the word.'

Her shoulders suddenly relaxed as she realised that what he suggested was impossible. 'That would be sensible…the starting as you mean to go on bit, I mean,' she agreed. 'But unfortunately my flat is tiny, one bedroom.' Her glance came to rest on his broad-shouldered frame. 'You wouldn't fit in…and I mean that in the literal sense.' She actually meant that in *every* sense.

'I am very adaptable.'

'Trust me, not *that* adaptable. My kitchen is about three feet square.'

'Compact.'

She gritted her teeth. 'The idea of slumming it might seem

amusing to you now, but I think the novelty would wear off rather rapidly.'

'You think I am spoilt? That I am incapable of roughing it?'

'Frankly, yes. When I said there was one bedroom...'

'Cosy.'

Her stomach muscles tensed. 'Very cosy with Nicky's bed in there too.'

'Nicky shares a room with you?'

She nodded. 'And I don't need to turn my TV on; I can hear the one in the flat next door.' A sweet couple, but noisy. 'I can hear a door close, and as for what I can hear through the bedroom walls! Even with a pillow over my head...not that we'd—' She broke off, blushing madly.

'You don't think that our love life would be as uninhibited as that of your neighbours?'

She flushed and hissed, 'I'm really not interested in other people's sex lives.'

'You never used to be a prude.'

She shot him a look of anguished embarrassment. 'I'm not a prude,' she denied indignantly. 'I just happen to think that what goes on between two people behind closed doors should be private,' she said. 'As for uninhibited, I seriously doubt that anyone could be as uninhibited as you!' As a lover Angolos had been not only passionate, but inventive. Thinking about how inventive made the colour fly to her face.

Her agonised observation made his lips quiver. 'You never seemed to mind and I always considered you the noisy one. There was that sound...' Eyes half closed, he drew a deep, shuddering breath. 'You know the one I mean, when I—'

Georgie pressed her hands to her burning cheeks. 'You're disgusting!' she hissed. 'You probably *like* the idea of people listening.' She could cope with being embarrassed; it was being aroused by his taunts that she couldn't deal with.

He was oblivious—*she hoped*—to her internal struggle; her embittered accusation caused his white grin to broaden.

'I never found I needed to resort to other forms of stimulation when you were in my bed, *agape mou*, but I'm always open to suggestions. In fact, you almost make me want to share your flat. However, you are right: it is not a practical solution.'

She regained enough control of her breathing to be able to respond with simulated calm. 'Exactly, and three months isn't very long. You can still see Nicky during that time…take him to the park and so forth.'

The way Angolos felt at that moment three months was a lifetime! If he didn't get Georgette back in his bed, and soon, he might well explode. He would certainly be incapable of functioning.

There was not a shred of his rampant frustration in his voice as he responded. 'That would be one solution, certainly. However, I favour a less…passive approach.'

'What *approach* did you have in mind?' she asked suspiciously.

'I'll get onto a local property agent.'

'There's virtually no rental property in the area,' she inserted quickly.

He looked amused by her intervention. 'I don't intend to rent; I intend to buy.'

'Buy!' she echoed, startled. 'That's crazy. It's only three months. Think of the expense.'

'*Expense…?*' He looked amused.

'All right, you have money to burn,' she conceded crossly. 'But it takes ages to find a suitable house, let alone buy one.'

'If you want something badly enough you make it happen.'

Their eyes connected and she knew that she hadn't imagined the undercurrent in his voice, the one that had sent a prickle of heat through her body. 'Now,' he continued, adopting a businesslike attitude, 'are there any areas you prefer? Is the distance to your work a factor?'

Georgie sighed and decided to go with the flow. When Angolos made up his mind about something, it was the most sensible thing to do.

With any luck the agent wouldn't have anything suitable on his books.

The agent did.

Two days later they drew up outside their new home.

It wasn't until the moment when Angolos opened the car door and stood back impatiently waiting for her to get out that the enormity of the step she had taken struck Georgie.

She was going to move in with the man who had broken her heart.

Angolos expected her to share his bed. She wanted to share his bed. It was inevitable, so where was the problem?

She slid from the front seat and stepped out onto the gravelled forecourt.

'So do you like it?' He sounded impatient to hear her opinion.

She flashed him an incredulous look. Like the place...? It was gorgeous. Georgian, faced in local brick, it had a gated approach, swish circular drive and, as she later discovered, private gardens in the rear that led down to the river.

'You've bought *this*?'

'I would have preferred for you to see it first, but there was a lot of interest. I had to act swiftly to secure it. It's small, but you were right—there isn't much on the market.'

'*Small!*' She released a slightly hysterical laugh as they walked up the steps that led to the porticoed entrance. Her entire flat could have fitted into one small corner of the massive hall revealed when he opened the door. She swung back to him. 'It's massive.'

'It's workable,' he conceded. 'And it's basically sound. I hope you didn't mind that I bought the furniture *in situ*...

It is not something I would normally do, but it is only a stopgap.'

She was unable to repress a laugh. 'You have a very unique take on stopgap, Angolos.' She ran a finger over the back of a carved oak chair. 'And I like the furniture.'

'Would you like to look around?'

She nodded eagerly and followed him into the drawing room. As they explored she couldn't hide the fact she was enchanted with the place. A satisfied expression appeared in his eyes as she began to plan out loud what she would use the rooms for.

'This can be Nicky's room,' she cried immediately when they walked into a light and airy south-facing room on the first floor. 'It's big, but not too big, and he will just *adore* the garden.' She gazed happily through the window. 'I wish we'd brought him with us.'

'I'm sure he will enjoy his little friend's birthday party.'

Absently Georgie nodded. 'I can just see him on his little trike out there.' Without thinking about it she leaned back into Angolos's body.

The contact with the hard warmth of his body sent a sharp shock through her own that sizzled down to her toes. She stiffened and then allowed herself to relax.

After a moment his arms came around her, drawing her closer as they tightened across her ribcage. Georgie, aware of every hard inch of him, pretended not to notice. If she acknowledged the embrace she would be obliged to do something about it, and she didn't want to.

'I always wished that I could afford somewhere with a garden,' she admitted with a wistful sigh.

'You could have if you hadn't been too proud and stubborn to use the money in the bank.'

'I couldn't take anything off you when you didn't believe that Nicky was yours.' Still in the circle of his arms, she turned her head and caught a stricken expression on Angolos's lean face. An expression that vanished the moment their eyes connected.

Without thinking, she half turned and reached out. 'It's *now* that's important, isn't it…?'

Angolos looked at the small hand laid on his arm and the muscles around his stern mouth relaxed. 'Yes,' he agreed.

The smile in his eyes as he looked into hers made her own smile fade. The emotions she'd been working so hard at keeping in check flowed without warning over the barriers she'd constructed.

Angolos watched the tears well in her eyes and his expression grew alarmed. 'Are you unwell?' Bending forward, he brought his face to her level and cupped her chin in one big hand. 'What is it? Tell me?' he demanded with increasing urgency.

She shook her head mutely and managed to mouth a barely intelligible, 'I'm fine. It's just…' Mutely she shook her head. 'I wish sometimes.'

'You wish things had been different?'

'I wish things could be like this all the time.' With a sigh she let her head fall against his chest. 'Sometimes I get so tired…'

'Things will be better when you have help…a nanny.'

'Not that sort of tired.' She closed her eyes as he lifted her hair off the nape of her neck and touched his lips to the gentle curve of her throat. 'And I don't need a nanny.'

'We are rarely alone.'

'That's part of being a parent.'

'I'm not complaining. It makes stolen moments all the more precious.'

Georgie gave a low, broken gasp of pleasure as she felt his tongue flicker moistly over her ear. Things low and deep in her belly shifted and tightened. 'Is that what this is?'

'It's whatever you want it to be.'

The sensual promise in his voice made her shiver. Their

eyes met and suddenly she was scared. Her eyes dropped from his but she extended her hand to him. 'Come on,' she said huskily. 'I want to see what's through there.'

After a moment Angolos took her hand and allowed himself to be led through the door into an adjoining room.

Georgie stopped dead. This was obviously the master bedroom.

'I've never slept in a four-poster,' she said, gazing at the impressive centrepiece of the room with its heavy canopy and elaborate carvings.

Angolos's voice above her head had a strained, husky quality to it. 'It isn't something I have had strong feelings about—until now. Suddenly I want very much to sleep in a four-poster bed.'

'Me too.'

His breathing was audible in the quiet room.

Georgie was hardly breathing at all as she turned around and lifted her face up to him. His was a dark blur as his warm lips immediately came over hers, hard and hungry. It felt so good, it felt so right, and most of all it felt mind-blowingly exciting.

'I convinced myself that I was over you,' she confided against his mouth as the deep, hungry assault morphed seamlessly into a series of soft, biting kisses.

She felt the muscles of his upper arms bunch beneath her hand and he slid his fingers into her hair, pushing through the slippery strands to mould the shape of her head. 'And are you?'

'I'll tell you on the condition you don't stop doing what you're doing if you don't like the answer.'

'I doubt I could stop if I wanted to,' he retorted. His throaty laugh did not reach his dark eyes; they remained intense and hungry.

'I was only over you in my dreams…and actually not there either.' Her dreams had always been filled with Angolos.

She was barely breathing as he leaned forward and slipped the buttons on her shirt. His eyes held hers as the fabric parted.

'Take it off for me.' Arms folded across his chest, he took a step backwards and waited.

The sensual request shuddered through her. Her eyelashes fluttered against the flushed curve of her cheeks as she lifted her gaze to his. 'You want me to…?'

'I just want you,' he inserted throatily.

Her breath snagged in her throat as he added, 'I always did and I always shall. From the first moment I laid eyes on you I was bewitched,' he imparted thickly.

The air felt cool against her overheated skin as she let her shirt fall to the floor. Thrusting one hip forward in a consciously provocative pose, she stretched her hands behind her back until her fingers found her bra clasp.

Sexual challenge glittering in her wide-spaced tawny eyes, she looked directly into his eyes. 'This too?'

He swallowed and nodded.

Georgie didn't watch the lacy scrap fall to the floor.

She watched Angolos.

Her heart felt as if it were trying to batter itself out of her chest. Her breathing was fast and shallow, her mouth dry. They weren't touching but she was so aroused she could barely breathe.

As her pink-tipped breasts sprang free of their confinement his eyes dropped. She heard his sharp intake of breath from where she was standing and she simply dissolved.

In one stride he was at her side. He carried her to the bed and fell with her onto the mattress. Before her head had hit the pillow his hungry mouth was on hers. He pulled her under him and she moaned into his mouth, squirming, relishing the heat and weight of his body pressing her down.

'I can't get enough of you,' she gasped when his mouth lifted momentarily from hers.

'You can have as much of me as you want,' he promised throatily.

'Don't stop, I'm...' she protested as he rolled away and pulled himself onto his knees.

A slow, predatory smile spread across his face as he looked down at her pale body, naked to the waist. 'You really are the most perfect thing.'

He cupped one breast in his hand. The feverish lines along his cheekbones drew attention to the glitter of his inky dark eyes as they moved over her skin like a caress. 'You're softer and fuller,' he marvelled, his eyes riveted to the quivering rise and fall of her breasts with their tightly engorged nipples.

'A baby, breast-feeding.' She was afraid the admission would break the mood, but it had the opposite effect on Angolos, whose breathing became even more ragged and uneven as he started to rip off his own clothes.

Her pulse was pounding in her ears as she watched him through the screen of her lashes. Halfway through he changed his mind and, leaving his shirt hanging open, he began to slide Georgie's jeans down her thighs.

Georgie eagerly kicked her way free of them. The sight of his dark head outlined against her breasts was an image that had featured in her dreams on countless lonely nights. The reality, the scalding pleasure that convulsed her body as his tongue moved back and forth, relentlessly over the rosy areola, surpassed any dream Georgie had ever had.

As he licked his way down her stomach she tangled her fingers in his dark silky hair.

Angolos lifted his head when he reached the barrier of her underwear. He smiled, a smile of predatory promise as he watched her face. Georgie's eyes closed and a keening cry was drawn from somewhere deep inside her as he slid his fingers under the lacy material. She released a second long moan of naked pleasure as he slid a finger over her slippery heat and inside her.

'This is…I can't…Angolos, I need you…now…now…!' She reached up and grabbed either side of his shirt. A determined tug brought him down on top of her.

The skin-to-skin contact as her breasts crushed against his hard, hair-roughened chest was almost too good to bear. She moved and the searing pleasure created by the friction of his sweat-slick skin against her own wrenched a series of sharp whimpers from her dry, aching throat. Her head was spinning, her starved senses reeling from sensual overload.

They kissed with frantic hunger.

But there was only so much of the kissing and touching Georgie could bear; she wanted more, much more.

Angolos responded to her loud announcement to this effect by grabbing her hair in one hand and forcing her head back onto the pillow. She listened to the passionate flood of words that flowed from his lips. He seemed unaware that he was speaking in his native tongue and Georgie didn't care. The expression stamped on his dark, driven features told her everything she needed to know.

As he rolled a little to one side and tugged at the zip of his trousers her eyes followed the sound.

'Oh!' she gasped as she saw the hard column of his engorged erection brush against his flat, hard belly. Her body was flooded by a tidal wave of hot longing that made her feel faint.

Watching her reaction with glittering eyes, his own dark features taut and strained, Angolos kicked aside his pants and reached for her.

Lying on top of him, she took his dark head between her hands and kissed him. She let her tongue dart into his mouth and felt the satisfying pulse of his rock-hard erection grind into the softness of her belly.

'Theos…!' He groaned an electrifying raw sound against her mouth, and flipped her over. Parting her legs with hands that trembled, he slid into her in one smooth, thrusting motion.

'Look at me!' he instructed throatily. 'I want to see you...I want to see you feel me.'

Georgie opened her eyes; his face was a dark blur above. 'Anything,' she sobbed as he moved inside her. 'Anything. I'll do anything for you.'

CHAPTER THIRTEEN

GEORGIE and Nicky were installed in the house two days before the start of term. Angolos was called away on urgent business and it was all terribly rushed so when her father phoned out of the blue and offered to help, after she had picked herself up off the floor Georgie said, 'Yes, please.'

'I don't know what you said to him,' Georgie said four days later as she sat on the edge of the desk in the room Angolos had done out as an office.

The place was full of space-age technology that made her nervous and the room next to it was occupied by his PA, a pleasant young man called Demitri.

'But Dad was being *really* nice. Not a single snide remark…and he made admiring noises about the house.'

'Say…? What makes you think I had anything to do with it?'

'Well, the last time my dad backed down was…' She pressed a finger to the faint dimple in her chin and pretended to consider the matter. 'Let me see…*never.*'

'Nothing to do with me,' Angolos insisted. 'Maybe…?' he began closing the laptop in front of him.

'Maybe what?' she prompted when he didn't continue.

Angolos looked up, his dark eyes grave. 'Maybe he could see you are happy…?'

Without warning Georgie felt her eyes fill. She blinked and swallowed past the emotional constriction in her throat.

'Maybe he could,' she admitted quietly.

In reply Angolos simply nodded, but she saw the flare of fierce satisfaction in his eyes before he opened his laptop once more.

This was the closest either of them had come to discussing whether their arrangement was working out. For her part, Georgie was afraid that admitting out loud that things were going well would be tempting fate.

Of course there had been awkward moments, and she wasn't totally at ease with being around him, but there had been none of the *major* difficulties that she had expected— *not yet.* Maybe, she mused, there had been so few disagreements because they were both being terribly diplomatic...?

And for Georgie there was the added complication of knowing that if she started speaking without first carefully thinking about what she was going to say the *love* word might inadvertently creep out.

Such behaviour was clearly out of the question when your husband wanted you back in his life because you were the mother of his child, not because you were...well...you. She was sure that someone as controlled and in charge of his emotions as Angolos would not welcome overt emotional displays.

It made her cringe to remember how as a newly-wed she had been all over him like a rash—well, he wouldn't be able to complain about that this time around.

Nicky, on the other hand, wasn't trying; he was just being Nicky. He had had no problem accepting Angolos's presence in his life. Angolos for his part was touchingly eager to be with his son. Even the most cynical observer, seeing them together, could not doubt Angolos's devotion to the child.

'I'll leave you to it, then,' she said, sliding off his desk.

'No need to run away.'

'You're busy and I should...' Their eyes locked and she paused.

'Wash your hair...?' he suggested. His eyes touched the silky waves and he decided it didn't look as though it needed washing; it looked shiny, slippery clean. He felt the urge to bury his face in it and inhale at the most unorthodox of moments.

'There's no need to be sarcastic.'

'And there's no need for you to be so painfully polite. The only time you actually relax around me is in bed.'

She refused to blush at the allusion. At night she didn't have to watch her tongue because it was a well-known fact that people said things they didn't mean in the slightest when they were in the grip of passion. She meant them, of course, but so far Angolos hadn't caught on. And anyway he said some things he didn't mean too, once the lights were out. Fortunately she didn't take them seriously.

'I don't want to intrude. I'm still feeling my way.'

I know my way pretty well around his body.

'Anyhow,' she added, her colour significantly heightened, 'you're not exactly acting normally around me, are you? If you were you would never have sat and watched that weepie movie with me last night.'

'That was compromise, not unease, and I wasn't watching the movie, I was watching you.'

'Oh!'

'I like watching you,' he added.

Georgie licked her dry lips; her heart had started thumping very fast. 'That's really strange. I'm not exactly—'

'Shall I tell you what you are?'

Angolos had half risen from his chair when his assistant walked in through the connecting door with a computer print-out in his hand. He was speaking in Greek, and frowning at the page in his hand.

Angolos replied in the same language and the young man looked up, flushing darkly.

'Sorry, I didn't know you were busy. I'll—'

'No,' Georgie said, leaping to her feet. 'I was just leaving.' Carefully avoiding her husband's eyes, she swept out of the room.

* * *

The headmistress was flatteringly reluctant to accept her resignation, but when she saw that her mind was made up she promised Georgie an excellent reference.

'You've been an invaluable member of the team,' she told Georgie warmly. 'And we're all going to miss you.'

Georgie, touched by the genuine warmth, left the office close to tears. Part of her felt sad and scared that this chapter of her life was ending. She wondered for the hundredth time if she was doing the right thing...

The news spread around the staff room the way secrets always did and by the end of the day at least six people had asked her if it was true.

The next morning at coffee she made an announcement.

'Yes, the rumours are true. I've handed in my notice and I'm leaving at half-term. My husband...'

The rest of her rehearsed speech was lost as the room quietly erupted.

'Oh, didn't I mention I was married?' she said when the hubbub had died down. She gave them a carefully edited version of the events that had led to their reconciliation.

They all thought it was dreadfully romantic and wanted to know when they were going to meet the man himself. Georgie was deliberately vague and not encouraging.

'He's snowed under with work. I don't expect I'll see him much myself.'

She did see him only a few hours later; so did the rest of the school. He made quite an impression—*big surprise!*—as he strode into the playground with Nicky perched on his shoulders. About to go back in the building after her stint on playground duty, she ushered the last child inside and closed the door.

'Hello, sweetheart.' Her smile faded as she shifted her attention to the elder Constantine male. 'What,' she demanded, 'are you doing here?'

'Are you this stern with the children?'

'Nicky should be in nursery and,' she added grimly, 'they shouldn't have let you just take him. You could have been anybody!'

'Not according to staff there. They were of the opinion that Nicky and I were—what was the expression?'

'Two peas in a pod?' she suggested drily.

'That is it,' he agreed with a complacent smile. 'They were charming.'

'I've noticed you have a way with women of a certain age.'

His dark eyes danced with amusement as he clicked his tongue in reproach. 'Animals like me too and I am asking your permission to take Nicky here out of nursery early. That children's theatre group you mentioned, they are putting on an afternoon performance. I thought I might take him. Don't look now,' he added, 'but I think we are being watched.'

'Of course we are being watched!' Maintaining a fixed smile was making her facial muscles ache. 'Could you be any more conspicuous if you tried?' she demanded, eyeing his tall, supremely elegant figure with exasperation.

'Is there something wrong with the way I look?'

Her eyes skimmed his tall, powerful body; he looked in-credible, but no more incredible than he always did. Dark jeans that matched the cashmere sweater he wore clung to the powerful muscles of his long thighs. They were simple clothes if expensive, but when he wore them they became something special.

'No,' she gritted grimly. 'That's the problem. Have you any idea what I'll have to put up with now? They'll all be talking about you,' she predicted gloomily.

They were, and more than a few envious glances were cast in her direction.

She smiled through the questions, the favourite being: 'He's gorgeous. How on earth did you catch him?' To her relief as the term progressed the excitement and teasing died down, though when Angolos appeared to collect her or Nicky he always caused a minor sensation amongst staff and mothers alike.

To Angolos she grumbled about their behaviour; privately she understood it—didn't her own pulses leap every time she saw him…?

It wasn't until the landlord contacted Georgie and said he had a new tenant for her flat that she realised she still had several boxes of her stuff sitting there. He went on to explain he needed her to clear the place by the end of next week.

'You really don't mind?' she asked the next day as she climbed into the Transit she had borrowed from the school secretary.

'You kidding?' Her friend Alan said, swinging Nicky high above his head, much to the child's delight. 'We're going to have a ball. Isn't *Daddy* helping you move out?'

Georgie grimaced; she didn't want to get into this.

Alan had made no secret of the fact that he thought her decision to move back to Greece with Angolos was crazy. 'The guy made you as unhappy as hell the first time, Georgie!'

But, being Alan, once he had said what he thought he had been as supportive as ever.

'Don't start, *please*,' she appealed to her friend with a warning look in Nicky's direction. 'Angolos is in Athens; he's not back until tomorrow.'

She had expected to be able to empty the flat in one go, but when the Transit was full there were still half a dozen boxes sitting there. She left with the intention of picking them up after school the next day.

Around lunch-time she received a call from Alan who offered to pick the stuff up for her.

She gratefully accepted the offer. 'That would be brilliant. I've got a parents' night after school that I totally forgot about and—'

'Just call me your guardian angel. Key in the usual place?' he asked cheerfully. 'And remember you owe me a pint.'

'At least,' she laughed. 'Do you mind keeping the stuff at your flat until tomorrow?'

'No problem.'

The parents' evening went on longer than usual and it wasn't just Nicky who felt cranky by the time they left for home. Her fatigue suddenly lifted as she saw the top-of-range Mercedes that Angolos drove parked in front of the house.

He was home early.

It was with a strange mixture of excitement and trepidation that she entered the house. The indomitable Emily, Angolos's half-Scots half-Greek ex-nanny, who, despite Georgie's initial doubts, was fast becoming indispensable, stepped into the brightly lit hallway as they walked in.

'You look exhausted.'

'It's been a long day,' Georgie admitted.

'Why don't you go and put your feet up? I'll give the little one his supper and bath.'

'Would you?' Georgie sighed. 'That would be marvellous,' she admitted, handing Nicky over into the other woman's capable hands. 'The car…?'

A broad smile spread across the older woman's homely features. 'He's in the study, dear.'

Georgie paused outside the study door and glanced at her flushed reflection in the mirror. The face that stared back at her was lit up from within.

His back to her, Angolos was looking out of the window. Despite her rigidly enforced restraint, she couldn't help the way her senses thrilled at the sight of his broad-shouldered, narrow-hipped figure.

'This is a surprise. I didn't expect you until much later.' Amazingly—at least it amazed her—nothing of what Georgie was feeling seeped into her voice.

'Obviously.'

The moment he opened his mouth she knew something was wrong. When he spun around to face her she saw she had not been mistaken...Angolos was in a foul humour.

'What's wrong?' She slid her bottom onto the arm of a chair and gave a sympathetic grimace. She lifted her hands to the log fire crackling in the hearth. The warmth it threw off didn't compensate for the inexplicable iciness in Angolos's manner. 'Did your meetings not go well?'

'I cancelled them,' he said curtly.

Her eyes widened. She knew from what he had told her they had been important—very important. 'Why?'

'Because I couldn't bear to be away from my loving wife.'

Hurt, Georgie flushed. 'Don't tell if you don't want to, I was only trying to take an interest. There's no need to be sarcastic.'

'Where have you been...or should I not ask?'

The question and his attitude brought a bewildered expression to her face. 'Of course you can ask. Do you have to pace around like that?' She watched him; how could she not? Everything he did, including pacing like a caged tiger, was rivetingly graceful.

One brow lifted to a satirical angle as his unfriendly dark eyes raked her face. 'I'm sublimating...what I actually want to do is wring your faithless neck.'

Georgie looked at him in astonishment. 'I've not the faintest idea what you're talking about, but I know I've had enough of this,' she said, getting to her feet. 'And you,' she flung over her shoulder.

'Don't walk away while I'm talking to you!'

She swung back. 'You're not talking, you're yelling at me, you're glowering and you're being generally incredibly unpleasant. But you're not talking to me.' She lifted a hand to her head in an intensely weary gesture. 'Shall I tell you something funny? When I saw your car I was excited...happy.' She stopped, hating the wobble in her voice.

'He didn't ring you, then. I thought he would...'

'*He...?*'

'*Theos!*' he raged, raking an unsteady hand through his hair. 'I may act like a fool where you are concerned, Georgette, but I would not advise you to treat me like an idiot,' he recommended in a low, throbbing voice.

'I've no idea what you're talking about,' she protested.

'I am talking—' he began advancing towards her with a slow, measured tread that reminded her of a panther menacing its prey '—about my visit to your flat.'

'You visited my flat...?'

Angolos watched her face; surprise but not the faintest trace of guilt was written there. He frowned as if her response was not what he had anticipated. 'You're a much better actress than I gave you credit for.'

'I take it that wasn't a compliment...'

He sucked in his breath through flared nostrils but didn't deign to respond to her comment.

'Why,' she asked, feeling her way, 'did you go to my flat?'

'I went because a person who said he was your landlord rang and said you still had property there and you had promised to vacate by today...but the why is not important—'

'*Today!* I've got until the end of the week!' she exclaimed indignantly. 'I'm sorry you had the bother. Alan's going to pick it up for me.' Surely the fact he had had a wasted journey could not account for his atrocious mood.

He shot her a look that simmered with hostility. 'So I understood from him.'

A sliver of caution crept into her manner; the antipathy Alan felt for Angolos was fully reciprocated. 'He was there...?'

'Oh, yes...he was there.'

She sighed. 'I suppose things got a little awkward?'

His brows lifted. '*Awkward...?*'

'Well, I know you never took to him...'

A choking sound emerged from Angolos's brown throat. 'And this surprises you?' he enquired.

'Not really,' she conceded with a sigh. 'But I wish you'd make a bit of an effort. Actually it's just as well he was there or you wouldn't have been able to get in. You don't have a key.'

'I must admit that I had not quite realised my good fortune until this moment.'

The inflection in his voice made her wince. 'Please don't be like that. I've had an awful day.'

In the act of raking his fingers through his hair he stopped and grabbed a hank of the dark silky strands in his clenched fingers. 'Mine hasn't been too terrific.'

'Do you want to talk about it?'

Her attempt to be an understanding wife was greeted with a look so hostile that she physically recoiled. 'I'll take that as no, shall I? Did Alan leave a message?'

'*No!*' The explosive negative emerged with the force of a bullet leaving a pistol. 'He did not leave a message and unless he is even more stupid than I think do not expect to hear from him any time soon.'

'You were horrible to him, weren't you? I'm going to have to ring him and apologise now.'

'*Apologise…?*' he echoed hoarsely, incredulous. 'Apologise for me?' His outraged gaze locked onto her. 'You will not apologise for me. In fact you will not speak to that man again. Nor will you see him. I made it very clear to your…Alan…that if he comes anywhere near you I will break every bone in his body!'

'You did *what*? Are you mad?' she demanded. No other immediate explanation sprang to mind for his extraordinary behaviour.

His lips twisted as he gave her question a moment's consideration. 'There is every possibility I am mad. I'm mad because I married you and I'm mad because I didn't break his neck. Nevertheless, I think the spineless jerk got the message. He knows what I'll do if I find him creeping around you again.'

She went white with a combination of fury and shock.

'Oh, for goodness' sake!' She was literally shaking with outrage as she stepped right up to him. 'Do you think this sort of stuff intimidates me?'

Angolos's eyes remained glued to the finger that was being jabbed into his chest.

'Because I can assure you it doesn't. It just shows you up for the nasty bully you are. How dare you sneer at my friends? And what makes you think you can tell me who I can or cannot have as a friend...?' She closed her eyes and shook her head. 'And to think I thought this might actually work!'

'What really offends me is that you brought my son in contact with that man!'

Eyes closed, she shook her head slowly from side to side. 'Contact? Nicky has known Alan all his life. He's marvellous with him.' Her eyes blinked open, bright gold and filled with sick, shocked comprehension. 'That's what this is about, isn't it? I thought you were a lot of things, but I never had you down as homophobic. Well, I don't care about your prejudices, but I won't have you pass them on to Nicky.

'For your information, Alan has been a good friend to me over the years and I don't intend to give him the push just because you're a nasty, narrow-minded bigot!' she finished breathlessly.

Angolos did not react to her impassioned outburst immediately. He didn't just not react—he didn't do anything. Not even an eyelash flickered as he stood there motionless, his dark liquid eyes trained on her face.

'What did you just say?' There was a strained quality to his accented voice.

'I don't remember,' she admitted miserably. The emotional aftermath of her outburst had left her literally shaking.

'*Homophobic…?*'

'Well, can you deny it?'

'Of course I can damn well deny it!'

'Really?' She gave a sceptical sniff. 'Well, what other reason could you possibly have for the way you're acting? *Well…?*' she added as he showed no signs of responding to her challenge.

Actually closer inspection revealed that his skin had acquired an unhealthy greyish tinge and the tension that held every muscle of his body rigid was scary.

'Are you all right?' she asked, her voice roughened by a concern she felt awkward revealing. In the space of seconds she had gone from wanting to hit him to wanting to hug him… She doubted there was another person in the world capable of drawing such an exhausting, extreme response from her.

Without saying anything, he walked over to his desk and opened the big diary that lay there. For several tense moments he stood there staring at the blank page. Still staring at the page, he said, 'I thought he was your lover.'

At first she thought she had misheard him. '*What…?*'

A great sigh shuddered from the depths of his chest as his eyes lifted to hers. 'I thought you were sleeping with the guy. What else was I to think?' he demanded, suddenly angry. 'He had a key and wherever you are he always turns up…'

'That's what friends do,' she reminded him. 'But he's gay.'

He slanted her a look that seethed with frustration. 'I know that now, but quite obviously *he* didn't know when he was in Greece.'

'You thought that I was sleeping with another man?' She lifted her eyes to his face expecting him to deny it. He didn't. She gave her head a tiny shake. 'This is mad…' she contended huskily. 'How on earth could you have thought even for one minute that…Alan…?'

'Stop this, Georgette.' The anger seemed to have drained

from him, leaving only a sense of immense weariness. 'I know what went on between you in Greece.'

'What are you talking about, *what went on*? I don't understand.'

Angolos studied her bewildered face and released a hard laugh. 'Then I'll explain, shall I? It means that you can stop pretending.'

'I'm not—'

'*Enough!*' His voice was like a clap of thunder. 'I found the note he wrote you. The day you told me you were pregnant.' He closed his eyes and quoted in a flat voice. '"I'm sorry. I thought I was ready, but I'm not. Sorry I'm not strong, love you always, Alan."'

'You remember it word for word?' Georgie was amazed by his perfect recall.

'Of course I bloody remember it word for word. I had the damned thing in my pocket when you told me you were pregnant. To me it seemed obvious that your lover had let you down so you were trying to pass off his baby as mine, because I knew that I couldn't father a child.'

Georgie stood stock-still, unable to believe what she was hearing. He scanned her marble-pale face and gave a twisted smile.

'But you could,' she whispered.

'Yes, I could. As a matter of interest, did you know who was the father before Nicky was born? Or were you relieved to have the matter settled when he looked so like me?'

Tears formed in Georgie's eyes. Not of anger—she had gone way past anger by this point. 'Yes, I knew who the father was. There was never any question of who the father was.'

'No contraception is foolproof,' he stressed.

It took several seconds for his meaning to sink in. For reasons that were now obvious, Angolos had never used contraception and had changed the subject whenever she had awkwardly broached it.

'I suppose I should be grateful you had safe sex.'

'Right now I want very badly to hit you.'

Angolos looked slightly disconcerted by her low comment voiced in an almost conversational tone.

'Alan came out to Greece because I asked him to. I was lonely.'

An explosive sound erupted from Angolos's throat as he began to stride towards the door. 'Are you trying to rub my nose in this, Georgette? Because—'

'What I'm trying to do is set the record straight,' she cut in. 'That letter you memorised would read slightly differently if you knew that I had persuaded Alan, or I thought I had persuaded him, to tell his parents about his sexuality.'

His back turned to her, Angolos froze. Slowly she saw his fingers unpeel from the door handle.

'He decided at the last minute that he couldn't go through with it,' Georgie told his broad back. 'It was another six months before he confronted them, and you know what was funny...?' She paused and brushed away the tears that were silently streaming down her face. 'They knew all the time. They had been waiting for him to tell them. Now you have to admit that that is classic.'

Angolos turned. The strain etched in the strong lines of his face was echoed in his eyes. 'Is this true?' he asked hoarsely. 'You were never lovers?'

'You're the only man I've ever slept with. My secret lover was only ever a figment of your sordid imagination.'

The accusation made the last dregs of colour leach from his face. The knuckles on the fist he had clenched against his mouth went white. With his other hand he wiped away the sheen of moisture from his forehead, but almost immediately beads of sweat bubbled up to replace it.

'What have I done?' He swallowed convulsively and

pressed his hands to his head. 'I thought you had made a fool
of me... My damned pride. I thought another man had given
you what I couldn't.'

Georgie stood there. She knew that seeing him go through
such agonies of remorse should be making her feel better, but
it wasn't. Seeing him suffer gave her no glow of satisfaction
at all. It just made her feel wretched, because when Angolos
hurt so did she.

Angolos's shoulders suddenly straightened. He looked directly at her. 'I will of course apologise to your friend.'

All her instincts made her want to run to him and throw
her arms around him, but his manner was so distant and formal that such a thing was unthinkable.

'Thank you.' She didn't know what else to say.

He shot her a pained look. 'You don't have to thank me.
Because of me you have spent the last three years struggling
to bring up a child alone.'

'It wasn't a struggle, it was a pleasure, and I wasn't alone,
I had my family.'

'I will make it up to you. If it takes me the rest of my life
I'll make it up to you,' he vowed, grinding one clenched fist
into the other.

'You think I want our marriage to be a penance?' She let
her head loll back to release some of the tension in her neck
muscles.

'What do you want our marriage to be?'

At last a question that she actually knew the answer to
without three hours' soul-searching. 'What I always wanted
it to be: a partnership of equals.' *Loving* equals, she silently
qualified.

He studied her in amazement. 'You still want that?'

'What has changed?'

Angolos stared at her, as far as he was concerned, everything had.

Five minutes earlier he had been comfortably occupying

the moral high ground. She had betrayed him but he had been prepared to put that to one side in order to preserve their marriage and create a stable home for their son.

Now he knew everything he had been thinking had been based on a lie. He had punished the woman he loved because he had been blinded by jealousy.

'I hope one day you will be able to forgive me for what I have done.'

'I do…'

'That isn't possible.'

She gave an exasperated sigh. 'Will you stop telling me how I feel? You're as bad as my family. It's true,' she added as he looked about to protest. 'You are. I know you feel bad, but that's not the important thing, is it…?'

'It isn't…?'

'We got back together because of Nicky, didn't we?'

Angolos, who was pacing restlessly around the room, stopped mid-stride. His face turned to hers; his dark eyes moved over her pale but resolute face. 'Is that why we got back together?'

She put down the strangeness of his tone to the discovery she had not been unfaithful. 'Well, obviously.'

He suddenly flopped down into an armchair. 'Of course it is.'

'Well, given that, does any of this really matter? You were wrong but the fact remains you can't change the past. So shouldn't we be concerned about making the future we want for our son? I'll sleep with someone if that will make you feel better.'

The smile died on her lips as he rose with one fluid motion to his feet, his face contorted in a mask of livid fury. 'No that would not make me feel…*better*.'

'For heaven's sake, Angolos, it was just a joke. You don't think I'd actually…well, no, you do think I'd…' She stopped and closed her eyes in despair. This was all coming out wrong.

Her eyes flickered open as she felt the light touch of his hands as they closed over her shoulders. 'So you want us to stay together for Nicky?'

I want us to stay together for us... 'Well, we can't give up at the first little problem, can we?'

'Little problem,' he repeated. 'You really have a novel outlook on life.'

'I have a practical outlook on life.'

'So we will do the practical thing and stay together.'

She nodded. She had got her own way and suddenly all she wanted to do was cry her eyes out.

CHAPTER FOURTEEN

THEY arrived at Paul and Mirrie Radcliff's the day before the christening, and were shown to the pretty guest room. It was charming and Nicky was equally happy with his camp-bed, which had been put up in the adjoining dressing room. Watching him playing with the Radcliffs' dog, a large animal of very mixed ancestry, Georgie wasn't at all surprised when Nicky introduced the subject of a dog of his own.

Angolos entered their bedroom as she was fastening the antique pearl choker around her neck. A glance in the mirror told her it was the exact finishing touch the outfit she'd brought for the christening needed.

'I suppose you know that Nicky thinks you're a soft touch. Damn,' she muttered as the catch eluded her. Angolos's silent scrutiny made her clumsy.

'*A soft touch...?*' She was soft...thinking of her softness made him hard. Around Georgette his normal self-control was non-existent.

Watching him lever his long, lean frame from the wall, she doubted that there was an adjective *less* appropriate. Everything about him was hard, including his impenetrable expression. He wore that expression a lot just lately. The only time he was spontaneous was in bed!

'Nicky says you said he can have a dog...a big dog,' she added drily.

'A boy should have a dog.'

'Did you?' she asked, giving up on her attempts to master the clasp as her arms began to ache.

He shook his dark head. 'My mother considered pets in the house to be unhygienic. But do you have any objections...?'

154

'No, I don't mind a few dog hairs on the furniture and I think you're right—a boy should have a dog.'

'You think I'm right? Be careful, Georgette,' he mocked. 'This is getting to be a habit. Let me,' he added, taking the choker from her unresisting clasp.

She stiffened as he brushed her hair from the nape of her neck, then as his fingertips brushed her skin she released a long, sibilant sigh.

'Problem?' he asked.

The enquiry made her eyes snap open. He had to know what his touch did to her. 'Give that to me,' she snapped, snatching the pearls from his grasp.

Hands up, Angolos took a step backwards. 'What did I do…?'

Georgie observed this display of bewilderment with exasperation. 'Nothing, that's the point,' she admitted, succumbing to a bout of ill-timed frankness. 'You don't have to do anything, you just,' she emphasised, stabbing her finger accusingly at him, 'have to be…*you*,' she finished lamely.

'Who would you like me to be? Do you find living with me such a burden?' he asked in a driven undertone.

'It's driving me crazy!' she admitted. 'Breathing the same air as you drives me crazy.'

'Then there is no more to be said.'

His air of cool finality made her want to scream. 'There's a great deal more to be said,' she yelled. 'I'm fed up with walking into a room and you not looking at me. The only place you want me is in bed,' she accused.

An expression of total astonishment swept across his face. 'That is totally untrue!'

'*I don't think so,*' she retorted bitterly. 'Did it ever occur to you that simply looking at you turns me to a…?' She suddenly buried her face in her hands. 'Look at me—I don't even know what I'm saying any more…'

Angolos, who had been staring at her, suddenly shook his

head as though to clear his thoughts. 'I am looking at you. I'm always looking at you... I can't stop looking at you. I want to touch you.'

The catch in his deep, driven voice penetrated her misery. Blinking, Georgie lifted her head. 'You only have me in the house because Nicky and I are a joint package.'

His jaw tightened. 'That is a ludicrous thing to say... At times,' he told her through gritted teeth, 'I could shake you. *You're my wife.*' He grasped her chin in his hand and drew her face up to his. 'I shouldn't have to apologise for wanting to look at you, but I feel as if I do.'

'I'm your mistress,' she contended stubbornly, 'in all but name—you only want me in your bed!' she accused.

'Sure, I want you in my bed. You in my bed is the only thing that's keeping me sane.' He dragged a visibly unsteady hand through his hair.

Georgie was mesmerised by the deep, hot flame that seemed to smoulder in his dark eyes.

'But I also want you to be my wife in every other sense. I just thought that since I... I thought that you would prefer it that way.'

Her lips quivered. 'Well, I don't,' she rebutted bluntly. 'Just because you're on some sort of stupid guilt trip and want to go around looking all stupidly noble I don't see why I should suffer.'

He looked disconcerted and slightly dazed by her forceful pronouncement. 'You are suffering...?'

She lifted her glowing eyes to his. 'Of course I am, you stupid man! I want to be able to talk to you about something that isn't to do with Nicky without being frozen out. I want to be able to yell at you, and hug you and—'

There was a knock on the door. *'Ignore it.'*

Georgie, who was struggling to catch her breath, was more than willing to follow his tight-lipped advice, but the second knock followed by an apologetic voice was harder to ignore.

Angolos cursed softly under his breath, said *'Later,'* and strode to the door.

'About time to go to the church, if you're ready...?' Paul, oblivious to the electric atmosphere, popped his head around Angolos and gave a thumbs-up sign. 'Looking good, Georgie,' he called cheerily.

Georgie, almost laughing at Angolos's expression, said thank you primly and promised she was ready.

Seeing Angolos with Paul and his wife had been a revelation to Georgie. She had never seen him as relaxed as he was in this informal setting. She had found it difficult to hide her amazement when she had seen her elegant husband roll up his sleeves and do the dishes.

The last of the guests left and Paul came out into the garden to join the two women, who were chatting cosily at the now deserted table. 'Well, I think that went very well...other than the Uncle Tim, vicar incident.'

'I think the vicar has heard the odd naughty joke in his life,' his wife laughed.

'Could be right. I heard he had quite a colourful life before he donned a dog-collar.' He pulled up a chair. 'Where's Angolos?'

'He's gone to check on Nicky,' Georgie explained.

'Right. Quite a live wire, isn't he, that boy?' He glanced down at the baby sleeping in the wicker crib set on the grass beside the women. 'I wonder if this one will be like that.'

'Worse, probably,' his fond mother suggested comfortably. 'Leave those, Paul,' she added as her husband began to gather up stray glasses. 'We can do them later. He isn't always so domesticated,' she added to Georgie. 'I think he's showing off for your benefit.'

'I like that,' said her indignant spouse with a grin as he dragged up a chair and proceeded to pour the last dregs from a champagne bottle into his glass. 'I'll say this for Angolos, he knows his wine, though I suspect most of our guests would have been just as happy with any old fizz.'

'Don't be rude, Paul—offer Georgie a drink. I know you've still got a crate of the stuff in the kitchen.'

Georgie raised her glass of mineral water. 'No, I'm fine, thank you.'

'When is it you move over to Greece?'

Georgie grimaced. 'Tuesday. I'm pretty nervous,' she admitted.

'Don't be. I'm sure you'll be fine. It's easy to see that you and Angolos are solid.'

'You think so?' Georgie asked, unaware of the wistful note in her voice or of the glance the married couple exchanged. 'To be honest I'm not Olympia's favourite person. Have you met…?'

Mirrie laughed. 'Oh, yes, we've met Olympia. Scary lady. But, Georgie, you're older and wiser now and, more importantly, you have Nicky. I predict that you've done the one thing that will grant you a place in that lady's heart. You've given her a grandson, lots and *lots* of Brownie points, girl. I think you'll find the balance of power has shifted.'

'I don't know about that,' Georgie said softly as she abandoned her seat and walked over to the crib.

Angolos emerged from the house just in time to hear her say, 'They're really lovely when they're this age, aren't they?'

'Worth all the hard work and pain,' Mirrie agreed, watching the younger girl with a thoughtful expression. 'And I had an easy labour, or so they told me. How about you?'

'Long,' Georgie said, her mind drifting back to those unendurably lonely hours when she had called out Angolos's name. He hadn't come and the doctor, whom the midwife had called when she'd become worried by the monitor readings, had been sympathetic but firm.

You can cry later; just now we need to get this baby out.

She gave her head a little shake… She never thought of

that. 'But that's par for the course with the first baby, so they tell me.'

The other woman grimaced in sympathy. 'Would I be wrong in thinking you're just the tiniest bit broody?' she probed gently.

Across the garden Angolos paused.

Georgie's head came up with jerk. 'Angolos doesn't want another baby just yet,' she said abruptly. Then, realising she'd made it sound as though Angolos had made the decision unilaterally, she added quickly, 'That is, we decided...' She lifted her slender shoulders in an awkward shrug.

'The mystery is to me that anyone ever has more than one,' Paul interjected, shaking his head. 'I know I couldn't do it again.'

'Do what, exactly, Paul?' his wife teased, winking at Georgie. 'Seriously,' she added before her husband could retort, 'I don't know what I'd have done in labour without this one.' Mirrie caught hold of her husband's hand. 'Just having him there to give me support made such a difference, but then I'm sure you know what I'm talking about.'

'*Mirrie!*' her husband muttered, elbowing her in the side.

'Ouch! I...' she began indignantly, then she saw Angolos standing there looking as if someone had just slid a knife between his ribs. His eyes were trained on Georgie, who looked equally stricken. Her hand came up to her mouth. 'Oh, I didn't mean...'

'Right, I think it's time to open another bottle,' Paul said, clapping his hands.

Angolos's gaze flickered to his friend. He exhaled the breath that had been trapped in his chest and smiled. 'Not for me, thanks, Paul,' he said quietly. 'But I wouldn't mind a coffee. Shall I...?'

'Are you saying I can't make coffee?' Beneath the teasing his friend looked concerned as he followed him back into the house.

*   *   *

Mirrie sought her bed early and Georgie wasn't far behind. The two men stayed up later, talking about, Georgie presumed, what men talked about when they stayed up late into the night.

Did Angolos discuss her? Did he talk about his marriage? Did his friend know that if it hadn't been for him discovering Nicky they would by now be divorced?

When Angolos did come to bed she lay there in the darkness listening. She heard him go into the dressing room, presumably to check on the soundly sleeping Nicky. When he came back the soft rustle of clothes indicated he was undressing.

'Did I wake you?' he asked when he slid between the sheets.

'How did you know I was awake?' she asked, her voice muffled by the pillow she was clutching to her chest.

Not that there was any chance of her falling asleep before he came to bed. Considering the fact she had slept alone for so long, her inability to sleep when he wasn't there was all the more perverse.

'I didn't.'

Georgie could hear the smile in his voice.

'Come here.' When he reached for her she allowed herself to be hauled up against him. She felt his breath warm on the back of her neck just before he kissed her ear.

'You're naked...' he discovered.

'I was hot.'

'This is something I have noticed about you,' he agreed.

She sighed and flipped over so that they lay chest to chest, thigh to thigh. She rubbed her cheek against his rough stubble. In the darkness a secret smile curved her lips as she felt his instant response.

He muttered something in Greek and then rolled away from her. A moment later there was a click.

She blinked as light from the bedside lamp illuminated the room. Her expression was a fair reflection of the seething sense of frustration she was feeling.

'What's wrong?'

'You have a very attractive pout.'

Angolos was lying propped up on one elbow, his eyes trained on her face. The sheet had slipped down to waist-level exposing each smooth muscle and hard angle of his taut torso. His skin gleamed like oiled silk in the subdued light. Georgie caught her breath as a spasm of sexual longing so intense she could taste it pierced to the core of her.

'We need to talk.'

'*Now…?*'

'Did you have a difficult labour?'

Georgie frowned and plucked at the sheet, pleating it between her fingers. It had been the very last thing she had expected him to say. 'Labour? What brought this on?'

He ignored her bewildered question. 'Was your grandmother there…or a friend?' He waited tensely for her reply; the idea of her being alone was intolerable.

She shook her head. 'Gran—can you see that? Gran's idea of being supportive would have been to tell me to pull myself together and get on with it.' When he didn't smile she added, 'No, I was alone.'

He closed his eyes and, alarmed by the expression that drew his skin taut across the marvellous bones of his face, Georgie pulled herself into an upright position, bringing the sheet with her.

'If you don't count a room full of medical staff.' *Where was this coming from?*

His dark lashes lifted. 'Do not make this a joke,' he reprimanded severely.

'I wasn't…' She released a sigh. 'I was just trying to…'

'Be very British and stoical,' he suggested.

This accusation drew a small smile from her. 'If you really

want to know I had a very long labour. Nicky was a big baby and I…'

Angolos's eyes followed the direction of her gaze and he added huskily, 'You are not.' *She was slender and delicate and…*

She nodded. 'That's what the midwife said,' she agreed. 'It lasted a long time.and I was pretty tired. I tried but… She got worried when Nicky's heartbeat slowed. The doctor was called.'

'The doctor,' Angolos exploded furiously, 'should have been there all along!' If he had been there he would have made sure that she had not been neglected. He caught her expression and made a visible effort to control himself. 'Sorry…go on,' he said tautly.

'There's not a lot to say.'

'You mean you don't want to tell me. I always know when you're hiding something, Georgette.'

If that were true, Georgie reflected, she was in big, *big* trouble! 'Not hiding, it's just everything was fine in the end. The doctor just thought it might be necessary to do an emergency section if things didn't move along.'

Georgie retained a distinct memory of grabbing the poor guy's arm and yelling, 'I don't care so long as my baby's all right.' The memory made her smile.

'But things did happen and it wasn't necessary.'

Angolos studied her in silence for a moment. 'You make light of it. I know you do,' he added impatiently as she opened her mouth to rebut the claim. 'But it must have been a terrifying experience.'

'I was very tired,' she admitted quietly. 'But a lot of women have it a lot worse than I did.'

'You were all alone and afraid.' Hand pressed to his forehead, he fell onto his back on the mattress. On the pillow his head turned towards her. 'You must have hated me.'

'Would it make you happier if I said I did? I don't know

why you're suddenly so determined to beat yourself up over this…it all happened a very long time ago.'

A spasm of self-disgust contorted his features. 'Of *course* you hated me!' A bitter laugh was drawn from his throat. 'How could you not? I rejected you and left you to give birth to my child alone. If I had been a bigger man I would…' Angolos flinched and turned his head to look at the small hand on his shoulder.

She simply couldn't bear the pain in his voice.

'You missed out too, Angolos,' she told him in a voice thickly congested with emotion. 'You,' she added swallowing, 'didn't see your son born.'

'And I will regret that to my dying day,' he admitted.

'I'm so sorry,' she said.

'Sorry…?'

Unable to bear the intensity of his scrutiny, she looked away. 'Yes, I am.'

A strangled expletive escaped his clenched teeth. 'The thing is you really are, aren't you? It's incredible. You haven't got a vindictive bone in your body.' Inexplicably—at least it was pretty inexplicable to Georgie—he sounded as though the discovery made him angry.

Georgie, thrown by his shift of mood, didn't know how to respond to this allegation. The silence between them stretched as his dark gaze seemed restless, but it always returned to her face. Sheet tethered in one hand, she reached across him for the lamp switch.

'Would you like another baby, *agape mou*?'

She flushed and looked at the big hand covering her own. The tender endearment was like a blade piercing her aching heart.

Not *a* baby; *your* baby.

Obviously she didn't voice her thoughts, though for a split second she had come close. How could she tell him how she felt when even she knew her feelings defied all logic? Turning her head slowly, Georgie met his eyes; his regard was too searching for her. Catching her full lower lip between her teeth, she looked away and with a sigh drew her knees up to her chin.

'That is a forlorn sound.'

'You heard what Mirrie said. I thought you must have.'

'And was she right?'

'We discussed this…'

'Did we?' he inserted.

'You know we did.' Her determination to convince him of her sincerity made her voice higher than usual.

'Maybe we should discuss it again.'

'I don't think so. Let's face it, our marriage is not what you'd call solid, is it?' Her laugh had a pretty hollow sound.

There was a long, dragging silence before Angolos responded. 'This is about our conversation earlier…?'

She shrugged.

'I am making you unhappy…?'

'That's not what I'm saying. It's just ours is a marriage of convenience. We're together for Nicky's sake. Sure, the sex is good…actually it is sensational,' she admitted, lifting her chin. 'But sex isn't enough.'

The problem was that, being with Paul and Mirrie and seeing what they had, that magical element…the fact was she had caught herself experiencing jealous pangs on several occasions. Was it greedy of her to want more?

'You're not getting all that you want from our marriage?' From the expression etched in the taut lines of his strong face, she assumed he was angry.

'It isn't about what I want.' She could never tell him what she wanted. 'A child should never be used to paper over the cracks in a relationship, and we have some gaping chasms. I mean, in case you had forgotten, if things had gone differently we would be divorced by now.'

'*Theos!*' he gritted. 'I am hardly likely to forget when you so obligingly remind me of the fact on a daily basis.'

'I don't...'

'Life is precious and, although it is clichéd, you should live every day as though it were your last. You live your life in the expectation of there being something cataclysmic around the next corner.'

'Maybe experience has taught me to expect things to go wrong.' The moment the bitter observation left her lips she regretted it. 'I'm sorry. I didn't mean to say that.'

He looked at the hand she laid on his arm and then looked away; a muscle along his jaw clenched. 'But you think it.' His dark glance swept across her face. 'Do not deny it. I am capable of accepting the part I have played in making you afraid to live life, *yineka mou*. Surely,' he added, 'the point is we are *not* divorced, and we are not going to be.'

'You can't *know* that.'

'Certainly I can *know* that,' he proclaimed. 'Unlike you, I am *totally* committed to this marriage.'

'Because of Nicky,' she said, as much to remind herself of this as to show him that she understood his motives and was all right with them. Actually she wasn't at all all right; actually thinking about him staying with her because of Nicky filled her with an inexpressible sadness.

'What other reason could there be, *agape mou*?'

Once again his volatile mood swing took her unawares. For some reason he sounded and looked utterly furious. She shrugged noncommittally, but on this occasion it did not lessen the intensity of the emotions he was projecting.

'The only thing that will take you away from me...' he reached across and framed her softly rounded chin between his thumb and forefinger; his other hand he fitted into the curve of her neck, pulling her close so that their faces were inches apart '...is an act of God,' he completed thickly.

He made it sound like a jail sentence. Was that how he

thought of it? 'I *am* as committed to this marriage as you are!' she protested.

He raked a hand through his dark hair. 'But it makes you shudder...?' He said it so softly that Georgie barely caught his bitter observation.

She laughed.

'What is funny?' he asked, with the air of someone who was very close to losing it.

Losing it was not something Angolos did often, but Georgie was far too preoccupied with keeping a grip herself to notice.

'Maybe the day will come when I can be naked in bed with you and not shudder when you touch me.' Her restless gaze roamed unrestrained over the firm, taut skin of his bronzed torso. She gulped and added huskily, 'But I suspect the day when you won't touch me will arrive a hell of a lot sooner...'

Angolos leaned across and pressed a finger to her lips. Georgie couldn't believe what she had just said, but she knew she had said it because he was looking unbearably smug.

'We were talking about extending our family, I believe? You agree that Nicky needs a brother or sister.'

'But you said—'

'Forget what I said. It is not a matter of not wanting. I felt that after being deprived of a father for the first years of his life Nicky deserved to have all my attention, but I have since come to realise that the best thing I can do for Nicky is give him a family life.

'A family life that involves all the rough and tumble and sharing that having siblings involves. The only problem I foresee is that addressing this problem will require me being naked in bed and possibly out of bed quite a lot.' He angled a questioning glance at her flushed face. 'Do you think that you could cope with that?'

Georgie managed to convince him that she could.

CHAPTER FIFTEEN

To GEORGIE'S amazement Mirrie's prediction turned out to be true. The dreaded Olympia took one look at Nicky and burst into floods of emotional tears.

As Angolos promptly walked out of the room, it was left to Georgie to comfort her. Suddenly Georgie found she was the flavour of the month. She had given her a grandchild— and he was a boy and there was no more talk of Sonia.

Georgie also found her mother-in-law easier to cope with when she lived ten miles away, though, as she doted on Nicky, she did visit frequently. In fact, the entire set-up was a lot less daunting the second time around. She could see now that half the problem before had been her lack of confidence.

Even though she was no longer that inexperienced girl she did have a few things to prove to herself, hence the party. For good measure she added Sonia to the guest list.

The day arrived.

What, she asked herself, possessed me? I'm not a society hostess. I can't do witty conversation… I'm not even totally sure what fork to use half the time. I knew all these things and yet I still thought it would be a good idea to invite a selection of rich, powerful people for dinner.

Clearly I have lost my mind.

The obvious solution is to cancel, she told herself. After all, it's not like I've got anything to prove.

Not much…!

She marched through the house to Angolos's study, and entered without knocking. She opened her mouth and saw he had his ear pressed to a phone.

Angolos motioned her to a chair, which Georgie sat down

in, feeling cheated out of her big entrance. The conversation was in Greek, but one word she did catch…*Sonia*.

She walked over to the wood-panelled wall and with a decisive motion yanked the phone cord from its socket.

It took Angolos a second or so to realise that the phone was dead. When he did he frowned and slammed it down on its cradle.

'There must be a fault on the line,' he began, turning, then he saw Georgie. He looked from the cord she was casually swinging back and forth to her face. 'Just what the hell are you doing?'

'Getting your attention.'

Angolos flopped down with fluid grace into a deeply padded leather swivel chair. He planted his chin on his interlaced fingers and looked at her through his lashes. 'You have it,' he promised.

'I came to tell you that I'm cancelling this dinner tonight.'

His brows lifted. *'And…?'*

His reaction threw her off stride. 'There is no and.'

'Right, no dinner.'

Her brows knit as she looked at him. 'Is that all you've got to say?'

'What else would you like me to say?'

'Don't patronise me!' she gritted back. 'In case it has escaped your notice I've been planning this dinner all week. A lot of very important people are coming and all you can say is, *Fine…*?'

'I said right, actually.'

'I don't care what you said.'

This contradictory statement caused him to massage the groove between his darkly delineated brows.

'I know you think I'm a total failure…I'm a social liability.'

'I never wanted the party anyway.'

'Don't humour me, Angolos.'

'I don't enjoy formal dinners.'

'Well, tough, because this one is going to be a great success!' As she slammed the door she could hear him laughing.

The preparations were going quite well when mid-morning she got a phone call.

'Emily, I've got to go out for a while. Can you hold the fort?'

She drove herself to the office and was ushered straight in. She brushed aside the offer of refreshment and got straight to the point.

'You've located my mother?'

The man looked at her with sympathetic spaniel eyes; he didn't look Georgie's idea of a hard-bitten private investigator at all. 'Your mother died two years ago.'

Georgie sank into the chair. 'I see…'

The sympathetic man handed her a thick file. 'It's all in there. She married the man who she…ahem. He is still alive; he owns a hotel chain and runs it with his eldest son.'

'Son! You mean I have a half-brother?' This was something she had not even considered.

'Yes, and two half-sisters. The details are all in there.'

By the time Georgie got back home her head was pounding. She had a family she didn't know, who probably didn't even know she existed. The choice as to what she should do with the information in the file was for later. Right now was for getting her head around the fact her mother was dead. It was silly—she hadn't known the woman and she still felt… Actually, she didn't know how she felt.

She would discuss it later with Angolos and see what he said, she decided.

Angolos had a lot to say, it turned out the moment she walked through the door.

'Where have you been?'

She was emotionally exhausted; his accusing tone was the last straw. 'Out?' she said shortly.

'Out somewhere with a man.'

Her eyes flew wide open. 'Pardon?'

'He rang to say he had something that belonged to me and, not to worry, he would make arrangements for me to get it back. When I asked who he was, he hung up. What was I supposed to think?' he asked grimly.

After this morning this was as much as she could take. She gave a contemptuous sniff and drew herself to her full height. 'The worst thing possible, I would imagine. After e…everything that has happened,' she added in a shaking voice, 'I can't believe you would still think that I would cheat on you. It was my purse that…'

'I thought you had been abducted…kidnapped…'

Georgie's jaw dropped. *'You're not serious…?'*

'I was within this…' he held his thumb and forefinger a whisper apart '…of calling the police.'

'But that's ridiculous!'

His response was a frigid, 'I'm glad you think so.'

A giggle escaped her compressed lips, then another and another…until she was laughing helplessly, tears streaming down her face.

Georgie's head continued to pound long after Angolos had walked out. She had not the faintest idea where he was or if he would even turn up for the wretched dinner party that night, and, she told herself angrily, she didn't care!

Actually the truth was she did care, and not just because the guest list for the dinner party was enough to make an accomplished society hostess nervous! Without Angolos to steer her through the evening the occasion would no doubt be a total disaster. And what was she supposed to tell them when they asked why he wasn't there?

She could see now that her laughing might have upset him; it had just been the shock of hearing him say what he had coming right on top of everything else that had set her off.

Angolos had been livid.

'Don't you walk away when I'm talking!' she yelled. Then, seeing her words had no effect on him, she added gruffly, 'When will you be back?'

He stopped then and looked at her through the mesh of his incredibly long lashes. 'When I can trust myself not to strangle you.'

Who knows when that might be? she thought gloomily now. From the way he had looked when he'd said it, it could easily be never.

With her personal life falling apart she had totally forgotten to tell the chef that one guest this evening was vegan and another had a dairy intolerance.

The chef, who had always regarded her with deep suspicion since he'd caught her making beans on toast one evening, received the information in silence.

At least, she reflected, he hadn't walked out too—not like some people. She hastily blinked away the tears that filled her eyes as Nicky appeared with Emily. He was wearing his swimming trunks.

'Oh, I'm sorry, darling,' she said, scooping him up. 'I know Mummy said she'd come swimming with you after lunch, but I'm really busy.'

Nine out of ten three-year-olds would have sulked at having a promised treat denied, but Nicky gave a philosophical little shrug that was heartbreakingly familiar.

She gave him a rib-cracking hug back. 'I promise I'll come tomorrow. Make him keep on his sun hat, will you, Emily?' she reminded the older woman.

'I will, my dear,' she promised.

It was half an hour later when she was giving her opinion of the flower arrangements in the formal dining room that Kostas the gardener rushed into the room unannounced.

'It is the little one!' he yelled.

'Nicky...?'

The man gestured towards the door. 'Come.'

Thomasis, the major domo, came up behind Georgie and spoke to Kostas in Greek.

'It is the little one,' he explained. 'Kostas says he slipped and hit his head on the side of the swimming pool. He is unconscious. I will call an ambulance…'

Before he had finished speaking Georgie was running. Halfway down the steps she ripped off her high heels and ran on barefoot down the flower-filled terraces that led to the tree-shaded pool area.

It was one of Georgie's favourite spots on the estate but at the moment she had no eyes for the panoramic views over the sparkling Aegean. Today all she saw was the tiny figure lying on the ground.

He looks so small.

'I'm so…sorry, he ran and…'

Georgie tuned out Emily's tearful explanation as she dropped down onto her knees beside Nicky.

'He's breathing,' she said as she brushed the tears streaming down her face away with the back of her hand. 'Thank God!' She touched the skin of his face and bit her lip. 'We can't leave him here; we should move him to the house.' She took his hand between her own and chafed it. 'Wake up, Nicky, sweetheart.'

'No, to be on the safe side I don't think we should move him. The ambulance will be here directly.' From somewhere Thomasis produced a blanket and tenderly placed it over the unconscious child.

'No, no, you're right,' she agreed. She screwed up her eyes as she made an effort to focus her thoughts. Despite these efforts all she felt as she spoke again was blind fear. 'Do you think he's…?'

'I think he's going to be fine, *kyria*,' Thomasis replied.

Georgie was vaguely conscious of Emily being led away weeping. 'He looks so small.' She took a deep breath and fought back the panic that threatened to overwhelm her. 'I want Angolos. He will know what to do.' She knew it was totally irrational, but she was sure that if Angolos were here he would make everything all right.

'We are trying to contact him,' came the soothing response.

The minutes while they waited for the ambulance seemed like a lifetime to Georgie and the journey to the hospital was a blur. She protested as Nicky was taken away, the language barrier made it worse and what little Greek she had acquired deserted her totally.

To her relief the doctor spoke perfect English.

After he had given her a consent form to sign and explained what they were about to do he looked at her marble-pale face. 'You do understand what I'm saying…?'

'Yes,' said Georgie, who had only taken in one word in three. 'Perhaps we should wait for my husband…?'

'I'm afraid that a delay would not be a good idea.'

Georgie swallowed. 'Fine, do what you must.'

When her mother-in-law made her sweeping entrance twenty minutes later Georgie was sitting there with her white-knuckled fingers closed around a cup of coffee someone had brought her fifteen minutes earlier. It was untouched and stone-cold.

Olympia wasn't alone; she never went anywhere alone. Her secretary, an elderly cousin who was her companion, and a liveried chauffeur accompanied her into the hospital.

By magic a comfortable chair appeared.

Olympia ignored it. 'I do not want a chair. I want to see a doctor. My dear,' she added, going straight to Georgie and enfolding her in a fragrant embrace. 'Have they told you anything?'

Georgie shook her head. 'They took him to Theatre; they said he had raised inter-cranial pressure. I think they're going to drill…' She couldn't bring herself to tell the older woman that the doctor hadn't given her a straight answer when she had asked if there was a chance of brain damage.

'*Theos…!*'

'How did you know? Is Angolos here?' Georgie asked her mother-in-law.

'No, I'm afraid we haven't been able to locate him yet, but do not worry, he will be here. Thomasis rang me. At a time like this you need family around.' She gave an understanding nod at the tears that began to silently run down Georgie's cheeks.

'You must put your faith in the doctors. They know what they are doing,' she said, gently taking the cup Georgie was still clutching from her hand. 'Sit down, my dear.' She looked at her daughter-in-law's bare feet but said nothing.

Georgie did as she was urged. She felt numb and strangely disconnected from the things going on around her.

'I want Angolos,' she said.

'Of course you do, and he will be here presently.'

'It's my fault…if I had gone swimming with Nicky none of this would have happened—'

'I do not want to hear that.' The imperious older woman cut her off mid-sentence. 'Accidents happen. There is no point in dealing in "what ifs". From what I have seen you are an attentive mother.'

The unexpected tribute brought fresh tears to Georgie's reddened eyes, but she knew that if Nicky's grandmother didn't blame her his father would. 'Angolos would never forgive me if anything happened to Nicky,' she predicted tragically.

'My son is a bigger man than that.'

'I know, but we argued,' Georgie admitted, biting her lip. 'He left; he was furious with me.'

The older woman took Georgie's hand between her own. 'Angolos is a man with a hot temper, but a big heart, and he loves you.'

Astonished, Georgie stared back at her mother-in-law.

'And I think you love him also…yes…?'

Georgie nodded.

'Then if you talk things will be all right. First,' she added briskly, 'we must find him, but I have people looking for him so do not worry. He will be here.'

And what will he find when he gets here…? Georgie hardly dared think that far ahead.

The two women sat in silence as the minutes ticked by.

'Why doesn't he come…?'

The rheumatic fingers around her own tightened. 'He could do nothing if he was here. Waiting is hard, I know…' The older woman heaved a sigh.

'What will I do if he doesn't get better? I can't bear…' Georgie's face crumpled. 'He's so little,' she wailed.

Olympia seemed to have no problem following this disjointed, sorrowful sentence.

'I thought we had agreed there is no point worrying about something that hasn't happened yet, and Nicky may be little but he is a Constantine and he is a fighter just like his father.'

'Yes, yes, he is, isn't he?' Georgie said eagerly. She gave a wan smile and wiped her damp face.

'And you are a Constantine now too, so you must be brave. Be brave for little Nicky; he will need his mother.'

Georgie swallowed and lifted her chin. 'Thank you,' she said thickly.

A nurse approached. 'Mrs Constantine?'

Both women got to their feet.

'Is there news?'

'Well, the doctor will explain, but…'

Georgie managed to hold back her emotion until she had spoken to the doctor and seen Nicky come round briefly after his operation. But when she left him sleeping peacefully again, then it all spilled out. She leaned against the wall, her body shaking with silent sobs as tears ran unheeded down her cheeks.

'Theos…!'

She opened her eyes and found herself looking up into the

dark eyes of her husband. Weak with relief, she staggered into his arms.

'Angolos!' she breathed as his arms closed tight around her. She felt his mouth in her hair; his breathing close to her ear was uneven and laboured.

'I'm so, so…sorry,' he said, his voice an agonised whisper. *'Is he…?'*

Then she realised he didn't know that Nicky had come through the operation and there would be no lasting damage. She lifted her head and took his face between her hands. The depth of pain inscribed in those proud lines shocked her deeply.

'Nicky is going to be fine, Angolos,' she told him. 'The operation was a total success.'

He froze, hope suddenly flaring in the shadowed depths of his eyes. 'But I thought, they told me, and when I saw you breaking your heart I thought he was…'

'It was relief; I was crying with relief.'

'This is true?' The big hands that took her shoulders were shaking. 'Nicky is going to be well…?'

She nodded, unable to speak past the emotional constriction in her aching throat. 'He was bleeding…' she touched her own head '…inside. They relieved the pressure.'

'Will there be any complications?'

She shook her head. 'No, they say he'll be a hundred per cent.'

She stood to one side and gestured towards the door. 'He's in there. Would you like to see him?'

The brown muscles in Angolos's throat worked as he nodded.

The nurse who was sitting beside the small figure whose head was swathed in bandages rose as they entered.

Angolos said something in Greek to which she replied in the same language. With a nod towards Georgie she moved away from the bed to make room for them.

'She said he'll sleep for a while yet,' Angolos said, his eyes trained on the sleeping figure.

Georgie nodded. 'He did wake up, though.'

'Did he ask for me?'

She shook her head. 'No,' she replied with a smile in her voice. 'He asked for a dog…a big dog and he also said that it wasn't his fault.'

The admission drew a short laugh from Angolos. He exhaled and dragged his long fingers through his dark hair. 'He looks so small.'

'I know.'

Angolos turned and looked at her. 'I'm so sorry,' he said thickly.

'*You're* sorry?'

'I wasn't there for you when you needed me.'

The self-recrimination in his voice made her shake her head in denial. 'But you couldn't know, and your mother was here.'

He looked astonished. 'My mother?'

She nodded. 'Yes, your mother, and actually she was pretty fantastic, a real hero. She stayed until Nicky woke up and then I made her go home. She looked exhausted; she left cousin Sabine with me.'

Angolos grimaced. 'That was kind of her,' he said drily.

Georgie's lips twitched. 'She is really a very nice woman.'

'She's a nitwit,' he retorted.

'She has a kind heart, actually, and she hates hospitals so it's very kind of her to offer to stay.'

'More like she's too scared of my mother to disagree.' Head turned slightly from her, he pressed the heels of his hands against his eyes. For the first time she registered the lines of exhaustion scoring his handsome face. The ache in her chest became a physical pain.

'I was going to get a coffee when you arrived. Would you like me to fetch you one…?'

At her soft words Angolos's head lifted. He looked at the

small hand curved over his arm and then at her face. A slow smile that made her heart flip spread slowly across his impossibly gorgeous face.

'Actually, I think I'll come with you. Nicky will not wake yet for a while…?'

She shook her head and turned to the nurse. 'That's right, isn't it?'

The nurse nodded.

'And if he does they've given me a bleeper,' Georgie added, producing the item from her pocket.

Angolos nodded and placed a hand on her shoulders and steered her towards the door. 'There are things we need to talk about.'

A finger of dread traced a path down her spine. *Oh, no…!*

'Are you cold?' asked Angolos, who felt her shiver.

'No.'

Up to this point Nicky's condition had been the only thing occupying Angolos's mind. Now that he knew Nicky was out of danger, Georgie, who knew the way his logical mind worked, knew that he would move on to the next obvious question—namely who was responsible for Nicky's accident?

'The café is this way,' she said when they got out into the corridor.

Angolos shook his head. 'If you don't mind I'll take a rain check. Hospitals,' he confided, 'are not my favourite place. Maybe we could sit outside…?'

'Sure.'

Angolos shot her an enquiring look when she hung back instead of following him.

'I know what you're going to say.'

His darkly defined brows drew together in a frown. 'That I seriously doubt,' he said drily.

'I do. And I just want to say that nothing you can say could make me feel worse than I already do,' she stressed in a tremulous voice. 'If I hadn't been busy with that wretched party

I would have gone swimming with Nicky as I promised and none of this would have happened.'

'If *I* hadn't flounced out of the house like an adolescent…if we had never met…'

She went pale. Was that what he wished…?

'You see how foolish and futile it is to think that way?'

'I suppose so,' she said in a small voice. 'I don't blame you for walking away. I was mean to you. The party was a stupid idea anyway. I only arranged it because I wanted to impress your mother and your friends and,' she admitted, 'Sonia.'

'Why?'

'Because I wanted to show you I was as good as her.'

He looked astonished. 'What on earth gave you the impression I wanted you to be like Sonia?'

'She's beautiful, and *she* knows what to say to important people, and your family thinks she was the perfect wife for you…also I suffer from terminal stupidity,' she added with a shrug. 'Actually I stopped caring about Sonia some time earlier this evening.' She took a deep breath and met his eyes. 'This morning I left my purse in the office of a private investigator I employed to trace my mother.'

'You did what?'

'I was going to tell you but there didn't seem much point if he didn't find anything.'

'And did he?'

She nodded. 'He told me she died two years ago and I have a half-brother and two half-sisters.' The words emerged in a rush.

He held open his arms and she walked into them. 'You did that all alone and then I shouted at you… I was frantic when I thought you were in danger. I'm so sorry.' She felt his lips in her hair.

'I don't know why I laughed…I just couldn't stop…'

'Hysteria, I should imagine.' He framed her face in his hands and turned it up to his.

The kiss was hard, hungry and at the same time breathtakingly tender. It drove every thought from her head.

'Oh, gracious,' she gasped shakily before he kissed her again.

When they disengaged he was breathing hard, but nothing else in his demeanour suggested he had done anything more extraordinary than say hello. Georgie's legs were shaking so much she could hardly walk but Angolos led her through a door and out into a quadrangle. It was an unlikely oasis of greenery in the middle of the miles of antiseptic corridors.

She touched a lemon tree. 'How did you know this was here?' She was pretty sure there had been no signposts in any language, and a person could walk this way a hundred times without discovering it.

'Insider knowledge?'

'Insider…?'

He nodded. 'It used to be just a few paving stones and benches. I had a landscape architect friend of mine make it over.'

'It's beautiful, and a lovely gesture, Angolos.'

She had already learnt that though Angolos donated generously to several charities, he did so on the strict proviso that his contributions were never made public. This, though, felt different. It was somehow…*personal*…?

'That door over there…'

Georgie's eyes followed the direction of his finger.

'It leads to the oncology unit.'

In her chest, her heart started beating fast. 'That's cancer treatment.'

His dark eyes held hers. 'That's right,' he confirmed.

'Did you know someone who was a patient here, Angolos?'

'In a manner of speaking. I had most of my treatment in London, but I did spend some time here when…well, I won't

bore you with the details. I was here for a few weeks on
and off.'

'You were ill?' The world started spinning in a sickening
fashion. 'You had c…c…?'

'Cancer. I had cancer.'

She looked at him, but his dark lean face—the face she
loved more than life—kept slipping in and out of her focus.
There had to be some mistake. Yes, that would be it—she
had misunderstood. Angolos was strong, he was… She was
not conscious of the choking sound that emerged from her
bloodless lips in the second before Angolos helped her sit
down on a slab of smoothly polished tree trunk.

'This is nice,' she said vaguely, running her hand along the
smooth wood that had been carved to provide a seat.

Angolos dropped to his knees before her.

'I didn't mean to shock you,' he said, taking her hands and
fitting his long fingers to hers.

She looked at their interlinked fingers. Fear was a metallic
taste in her mouth. 'You're well now?' she said, lifting her
terror-filled eyes to his. 'It went away?'

'It went away,' he confirmed.

A tremulous breath hissed from her parted lips. Obviously
it had; the man literally oozed vitality. 'When did it happen?'

'I had just been given the all-clear the day we met.'

She disentangled her hands from his and wrapped them
around her shaking body in a defensive gesture. This shock
fresh on the top of the previous one had an oddly numbing
effect. With her eyes closed she suddenly saw his beautiful,
fallen-angel face exactly as it had been that day.

'That's why you were so thin.' She suddenly turned accusing eyes on him. 'You jumped in the sea to rescue me and
you were ill.'

'Not as ill as you'd have been if I hadn't jumped in.'

'This isn't a laughing matter,' she rebuked. 'Oh, I should
have known…why didn't I know?'

'I had come down to give Paul the news.'

If it weren't for him… His shoulders lifted. 'Basically if it hadn't been for Paul I'd be dead.'

'Don't say that!' she pleaded. The idea of a world without Angolos in it was too appalling to contemplate. 'I always liked Paul.'

He grinned.

It suddenly struck her what all this meant. 'Basically when you met me you'd just had a death sentence lifted.'

'In a manner of speaking I suppose I had.'

'And you weren't what most people would call in your right mind… Oh, that explains a lot.' In fact it explained everything.

A dangerous expression entered his eyes as he watched her putting two and two together. 'What does it explain?'

'Do me a favour, Angolos. In your right mind you'd never have looked at someone like me twice let alone marry… No wonder all your family and friends disapproved.' She let out a weak laugh and covered her face with her hands.

He had got rid of her as soon as he'd recovered his senses and that situation would have been made official if he hadn't discovered he had a son. Why was she making this such a big thing? It weren't as if she hadn't always known that the marriage was all about Nicky.

Angolos took hold of her wrists and prised her hands away. 'Look at me!' he commanded.

She shook her head and heard his frustrated curse.

'Nobody goes through an illness like I did without it changing them, even profoundly changing them,' he conceded.

She lifted her chin. 'I'd say I can imagine, but I can't,' she admitted.

'It makes a man…or at least it made me,' he corrected, 'reassess things. I discovered that I didn't much like the person I had become. I was wealthy and what was I doing with my wealth? Making it grow… Yes, I'm good at making money, but was it making me happy?' He shook his head. 'I decided that if I got a second chance things were going to be different. Far from suffering from some sort of temporary insanity, I think the day I walked along that beach and saw you…I think that I was the sanest I had ever been.'

'Why didn't you tell me, Angolos?'

'Because I didn't want to see you look at me differently.'

'I wouldn't have…' she began to protest.

He looked at her. 'Are you sure?'

She sighed. 'Maybe you're right,' she admitted reluctantly.

'When you're ill people don't see the person, they see the disease. And some don't know how to deal with it; maybe it reminds them of their own mortality. With you there was none of that. They told me that the likelihood was the treatment would make me sterile. A trade-off, they called it. Basically I think the reason I didn't tell you was I knew you weren't really in love with me and I couldn't risk losing you, *agape mou*…I couldn't.'

The pain in his voice brought tears to her eyes. 'But you wouldn't have lost me, darling,' she protested. 'Of course I loved you. I always have and I always will.'

'I should have let you go… Hell, I tried, but I couldn't…'

'I didn't want to be let go. I wanted you.'

He shook his head. 'You were in love with the guy who saved your life. You were in love with a hero figure who could walk on water. I wasn't that man, but,' he added bitterly, 'I wanted to be, for you.'

'I didn't want a hero, I wanted a husband.'

'A husband who had had his body pumped full of chemicals? A husband who couldn't give you a baby? You asked me why I didn't tell you, why I didn't give you the opportunity to say, Thanks, but no, thanks.'

'I wouldn't have!'

He stilled her instinctive protest with a brush of his pain-filled eyes. 'The truth is—' He paused, swallowing hard, and

Georgie, who couldn't bear the pain and self-loathing in his voice, pushed her fist in her mouth to stop herself crying out. 'I knew if I told you the truth there was a good chance I would lose you. My behaviour from the moment I met you was totally reprehensible. I fell in love with you at first sight.'

'You…with me…' Somewhere inside her there were fireworks of pure joy exploding.

'Totally, and completely. I took advantage of your youth and inexperience. You were so young and I knew full well that what you felt for me was a crush. I knew you weren't ready for marriage…'

Georgie could hold her tongue no longer. 'That's the biggest load of patronising rubbish I've ever heard.' He blinked and she smiled at him with total confidence. 'I may have been young, but does that make what I felt any less valid? Angolos, I wasn't a teenager, and don't you think I'm in a better position than you to know if I was ready for marriage?'

'The truth is, Georgette, I was scared out of my mind of losing you,' he confessed huskily.

She brushed the tears from her cheek with the back of her hand and sniffed. 'Well, you're not going to lose me now,' she said firmly. 'You're stuck with me for ever and this time you're going to be there when this baby pops out.'

An expression of shock froze his mobile features. *'Baby…?'* His eyes dropped.

She nodded and, taking his hand, laid it on her flat belly. The feeling of his hand there warm against her was the best feeling in the world. 'Baby…I was sort of planning to tell you after the party tonight.' Her eyes widened in sudden horror. 'Oh, no, the party—all those people!'

'To hell with those people,' Angolos said with callous disregard for their comfort or her reputation as society hostess. 'A baby…now *that's* amazing.'

'Not really, considering the amount of effort you've put into the project. What's amazing is that you love me!'

He ran a finger down the curve of her cheek. 'No, what's amazing is that you can love me after all the pain I've caused you.'

'And all the pleasure, Angolos…all the pleasure. You gave me Nicky… Talking of Nicky, he's awake!' Laughing, she extracted the vibrating pager from her pocket and handed it to him. 'This is what life is like as a parent at the beck and call of children twenty-four seven.'

The prospect of this life illuminated Angolos's face with joy that brought a lump to her throat. 'I'm a man who thought I had no life. Now I have the woman I was born to love and a son and another on the way. What,' he demanded, pulling her to her feet, 'could be better?'

'A daughter?'

'That would be acceptable,' he conceded. 'Now, twins would be something…'

'Don't,' she begged, laughing, 'even *think* about it.'

'Shall we tell Nicky he's going to have a brother or sister?'

'He'll say he'd prefer a dog,' Georgie predicted.

Laughing, Angolos drew her to him. 'I love you,' he said, gazing tenderly into her happy, glowing face.

The future, Georgie thought, looked good, but she was content to enjoy the golden present. 'I love you too.'

'I loved you first,' he retorted.

'You always have to have the last wo—' Her husband silenced her retort in the time-honoured manner and Georgie… she didn't mind a bit!

0505/01a

Modern
romance™

MARRIED BY ARRANGEMENT *by Lynne Graham*

Spanish aristocrat Antonio Rocha viewed Sophie as a commoner – she was bringing up his orphaned niece in a caravan! Sophie might not speak or live like a lady, but she had plenty of love to give. Antonio found himself inexplicably attracted to her…

PREGNANCY OF REVENGE *by Jacqueline Baird*

Charlotte Summerville was a gold digger according to billionaire Jake d'Amato and he planned to take revenge in his bed! Suddenly innocent Charlie was married to a man who wanted her, but hated her…and she was pregnant with his child…

IN THE MILLIONAIRE'S POSSESSION *by Sara Craven*

Pretty but penniless Helen Frayne wants to save her ancestral home. Arrogant millionaire property magnate Marc Delaroche thinks Helen will sell herself to keep it – and he's proved right when she agrees to become his wife of convenience…

THE ONE-NIGHT WIFE *by Sandra Marton*

Savannah McRae knows that to help her sister she has to win big. But sexy Sean O'Connell always plays to win, and virginal Savannah is no match for him. Soon she has lost everything and Sean offers to help: he'll settle her debts if she becomes his wife – for one night!

Don't miss out…

On sale 3rd June 2005

Available at most branches of WHSmith, Tesco, ASDA, Martins, Borders, Eason, Sainsbury's and all good paperback bookshops.

Visit www.millsandboon.co.uk

MIRA®
An international collection of bestselling authors

EVER AFTER
by Fiona Hood-Stewart

**"An enthralling page turner—
not to be missed." —*New York Times*
bestselling author Joan Johnston**

**She belongs to a world of wealth,
politics and social climbing. But
now Elm must break away to find
happily ever after...**

Elm MacBride can no longer sit back and
watch her corrupt and deceitful husband's
ascent to power and his final betrayal sends her
fleeing to Switzerland where she meets
Irishman Johnny Graney. When her husband's
actions threaten to destroy her, Johnny must
save not only their love but Elm's life...

ISBN 07783 2078 2

Published 15th April 2005

MILLS & BOON

Volume 12 on sale from 4th June 2005

Lynne Graham

International Playboys

Tempestuous Reunion

Available at most branches of WHSmith, Tesco, Martins, Borders, Eason, Sainsbury's and all good paperback bookshops.

FREE

4 BOOKS AND A SURPRISE GIFT!

We would like to take this opportunity to thank you for reading this Mills & Boon® book by offering you the chance to take FOUR more specially selected titles from the Modern Romance™ series absolutely FREE! We're also making this offer to introduce you to the benefits of the Reader Service™—

- ★ **FREE home delivery**
- ★ **FREE gifts and competitions**
- ★ **FREE monthly Newsletter**
- ★ **Books available before they're in the shops**
- ★ **Exclusive Reader Service offers**

Accepting these FREE books and gift places you under no obligation to buy; you may cancel at any time, even after receiving your free shipment. Simply complete your details below and return the entire page to the address below. You don't even need a stamp!

YES! Please send me 4 free Modern Romance books and a surprise gift. I understand that unless you hear from me, I will receive 6 superb new titles every month for just £2.75 each, postage and packing free. I am under no obligation to purchase any books and may cancel my subscription at any time. The free books and gift will be mine to keep in any case.

P5ZEE

Ms/Mrs/Miss/Mr...Initials ....
                                                                    BLOCK CAPITALS PLEASE

Surname ....

Address ....

....

....Postcode ....

Send this whole page to:

The Reader Service, FREEPOST CN81, Croydon, CR9 3WZ